# A Land Apart

*To Rose*

*Written and Illustrated by*

Ian Roberts

Publisher's Cataloging-in-Publication Data
Names: Roberts, Ian, 1952 - author.
Title: A land apart / Ian Roberts.
Description: Los Angeles : Atelier Saint-Luc Press, 2019.
Identifiers: LCCN 2018902867 | ISBN 978-0-9728723-3-1 (pbk.) | ISBN 978-0-9728723-4-8 (Kindle
    ebook) | ISBN 978-0-9728723-8-6 (EPUB ebook) | 978-0-9728723-9-3 (ebook)
Subjects: LCSH: Bru   1            -1632—Fiction. | Canada—History—To 1763 (New France)—
Fiction. | Europe—Colonies—America—Fiction. | Wyandot Indians—Fiction. | Iroquois Indians—
Fiction. | Historical fiction.
    BISAC: FICTION / Historical / General. | FICTION / Native American & Aboriginal
    GSAFD:  Historical Fiction.
Classification: LCC PS3618.034 L36 2019 (print) | LCC PS3618 034 (ebook) | DDC 813/.6—dc23

Published by Atelier Saint-Luc Press
        200 South Barrington,  #202
        Los Angeles, CA 90049

Atelier Saint-Luc Press titles are distributed by Small Press United, Chicago (800-888-4741)

Printed in the United States of America.

10 9 8 7 6 5 4 3 2 1

*To the Land — that ancient, speaking presence.*

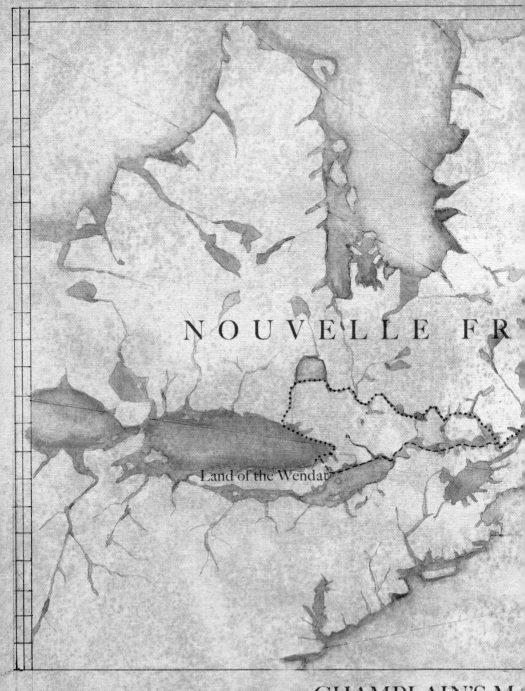

NOUVELLE FR

Land of the Wendat

CHAMPLAIN'S MA

C E

bee

North Route ··········
South Route ------

F NEW FRANCE 1632.

New France
1634

Part One

He strokes his fingers along the polished mahogany stock of the musket, caressing it slowly, the way a more sensual man might caress the skin of a lover. His hand curls around the cool black wrought iron of the barrel. The oil on the metal smells sweet. He hoists the musket to his shoulder, pulling the stock in tight as he had been instructed. Sighting down the barrel, he sees only wide-open lake. Slowly he pivots toward land. As the muzzle swings toward them, the English traders duck and scatter out of the way. The soldiers, standing to one side, anxiously raise their own guns in self-defense. Totiri ignores them all.

Staring down the barrel of the musket at a tree trunk several yards away, he pulls the stock in tight again, holds the barrel steady and slowly squeezes the trigger. The flintlock releases with a click and then three powerful, exhilarating sensations hit him at once: the kick of the musket hard into his shoulder, the deafening roar, and the dense, acrid smell of burnt powder smoke. The musket ball strikes the tree as the crashing echo of his shot rolls back from across the lake.

Slowly and carefully, the Iroquois war chief lowers the gun. Never has he experienced such a powerful sensory affront. He revels in its sheer intensity as he slowly regains his equilibrium. Totiri knew before lifting the musket that he wanted it; now the desire consumes him. He holds the musket tight in his grip, unsure what this power is, unsettled by it, knowing only that he is awed by its dark spirit. He looks up, suddenly aware once again of his surroundings. And the English, and his reason for being here — to trade furs for this thundermaker he now holds. But Totiri knows they've seen his lust. That is not good. That is weakness.

A British soldier leans towards a comrade, his eyes and musket at the ready, "Like baring your neck to wolves." His friend nods, aware of the tenuous and dangerous alliance they now forge. "I do not see any good coming from this."

Handing the gun to an Iroquois warrior beside him, Totiri turns his attention to the English trader. The tension between them is palpable. Totiri eyes the long, wooden cases filled with guns. And several more cases laying behind the traders. He wants them all. He nods at the furs his hunters have brought. The trader flips the furs with a dismissive gesture, implying their inferior quality.

Totiri snarls at the insult. The trader steps back, cringing despite himself, at the intensity of the man's anger. He has never encountered anyone like Totiri. The war chief bristles with a current of menace and cruelty. Battle scars cover his arms and chest. The trader knows he has the upper hand; he knows how much the Iroquois crave these muskets. He knows he mustn't back down, holding the war chief's gaze as long as he can. But he soon folds, unable to withstand the chilling hostility any longer.

This is barter and the trader knows he's losing. He adds two more kegs of powder and several boxes of shot. He tries to smile, but his fear betrays him, a line of cold sweat runs down the inside of his shirt, another down his forehead into his eyes. Totiri takes him in with undisguised scorn. Then, with the slightest hint of a nod from the chief, his warriors move toward the muskets, powder and shot. The six English soldiers hold their guns loosely at the ready, sensing the danger of the Iroquois suddenly as a group moving toward them. Totiri eyes each case and crate and when the last one passes, he casts a long, last look at the remaining cases behind the traders.

As the last Iroquois turns to go, one of the traders suddenly crosses his path, quietly handing him a small bottle of dark liquid. It is a movement Totiri does not miss. With two swift strides he grabs the bottle, pitches and smashes it on the rocks and strikes the warrior hard across the face with the backhand motion of his throw. As the trader stumbles backwards onto the ground, six soldiers raise their guns at the war chief. Totiri slowly lifts his gaze, staring with disdain straight into their muskets. He knows they wouldn't dare. He turns his back and walks with a deliberate, slow pace away from the white men, relishing their discomfort. He can smell it.

Four canoes of Wendat return, heavily laden
with furs traded with tribes to the west.

In the stern of the last canoe sits a Frenchman, the only white man who has ever ventured this deep into the wilderness, though little in his demeanor or appearance betrays those European roots. Etienne Brulé is about forty years old, with long hair, clean-shaven face, and deerskin vest and leggings. He looks as Wendat as his companions, at least to any European, except for his clear blue eyes. Scars from burns mark almost every inch of his neck and chest.

Paddling in front of Brûlé is his friend, Savignon, a Wendat of about the same age. He spent three years in France and it changed him dramatically. Although over twenty years ago some of that European influence is still evident even now in the French smock coat he wears, once a pale grey velvet, though now soiled, discoloured with both sleeves cut off.

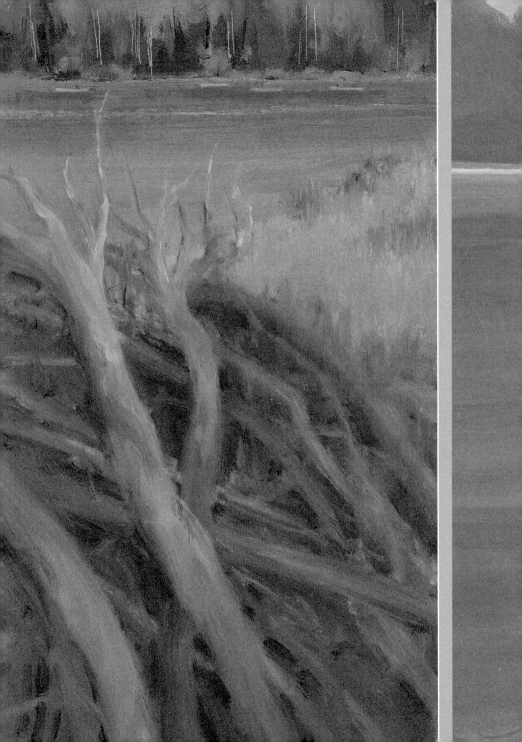

As they cross the clearing at the top of the portage, a breathtaking panorama opens up. In the afternoon light, the lake, like beaten gold, appears and reappears off into the distance. The two men stop, two tiny figures in a vast wilderness.

Brulé drops his pack, and slowly spreads his arms wide, breathing in the whole vista of the land before them, as if to embrace it into himself. He turns to Savignon, "This, my friend, is paradise."

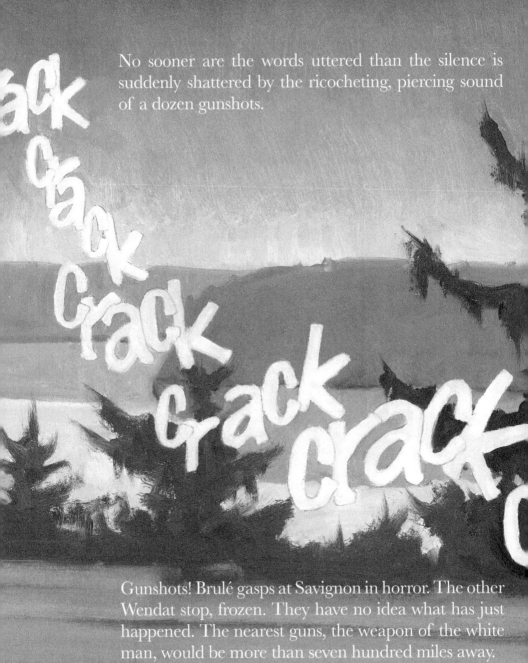

No sooner are the words uttered than the silence is suddenly shattered by the ricocheting, piercing sound of a dozen gunshots.

Gunshots! Brulé gasps at Savignon in horror. The other Wendat stop, frozen. They have no idea what has just happened. The nearest guns, the weapon of the white man, would be more than seven hundred miles away.

Smoke drifts out from behind a point of land far down the lake.

Brulé, Savignon and their Wendat companions run, almost glide, through the woods. They make no sound as they close in to where the gunfire must have come from. They can hear cries and shouts as they carefully make their way to a clearing by the water's edge.

On that silent sliver of shoreline lie a number of dead warriors. Smoke hangs over the clearing, and the burnt and scattered remains of their small fishing camp still smolder. Brulé looks up from the ravaged scene. Out on the water, Iroquois paddle away, their canoes riding low, crammed with the women and children of the dead men lying before them. The captives' cries and wails slowly fade as their canoes, one by one, round the next point of land and disappear down the lake.

No one utters a word. Never before has a Wendat seen a man killed by a bullet. Scanning the slaughter, Brulé pieces together what must have happened. The Iroquois had arrived silently through the woods and surrounded the camp. Then fired. Each warrior dropped where he had stood. Four men lay in the shallow water by the shore. Three must have still been alive where they fell. They had been given a final deathblow. Two had taken the first bullet and charged but were dropped with the one that followed. The attack would have been over in seconds.

Savignon turns over one of the warriors. "Chippawa," he says. "Iroquois allies. We have never had Iroquois this far west before."

Brulé nod,"For them to do this, to their allies, the Iroquois must hurt from the white man's disease more than we realize. More than it hurts us," adds Brulé.

A slight stirring behind them breaks the silence. As one, the Wendat turn, alert, clubs and tomahawks raised and ready. Brulé, standing to one side of his companions, realizes what has drawn their attention and relaxes. He calls out, "Hey, little man. You need not fear us."

Nothing moves. He tries again. "We will get you home. You cannot stay here."

From behind a tree, the frightened face of a young boy peers out. Brulé gestures to him to approach, holding out his hand. No more than four or five, tear-stained, dirty and almost naked, the boy slowly steps into the clearing. A bullet has grazed his side and a wide stream of blood flows from his wound snaking its way down his leg. Tentatively, he moves towards Brulé's outstretched hand. The white man pulls him gently to his side, resting his hand on the boy's head. He looks at the silent, grim faces of his Wendat companions.

Samuel Champlain, the Governor of New France, taps his finger slowly and methodically on his desk. He stares at the sunlight gently streaming through the small window of his office. Two men lean against the heavy timber wall of the fort, smoking their pipes in the morning sun.

Champlain is sixty-years-old and looks it. Wresting Québec into existence has taken its toll. For the last twenty-five years he has devoted his life to fashioning this tiny colony out of a brutal, uncooperative wilderness. Although New France in principle stretches over a territory fifteen times the size of France itself, it is only here in Québec that some semblance of colonization has slowly taken root.

Each year the promise of land and its riches draws the adventurers and dreamers out of France. One winter here and most beg to return home. Yet, the French government, despite all evidence to the contrary, stubbornly continues to believe that Québec will yield the kind of riches Spain discovered in their New World to the south.

Champlain can never quite anticipate what will arrive each summer with the supply ships that come from France once a year. But always when they discharge their cargo they also discharge new plans, new demands, or even a new governor to replace him — until the grim reality of running this place sets in and the newly-arrived find any excuse to head back. The French court, when they think of New France at all, envisions turning this wilderness into a kind of frontier Paris. Unlike them, he has learned through long experience here to temper his expectations.

When young, Champlain had spent time with the Spanish in the Caribbean and had seen the misery inflicted on the native people — not just the slavery but the pillage and murder. He had vowed to do things differently here in New France. He believed the French could live with the natives as one, in peace, assuming, of course, that they would live as one as Christians.

The Algonquin, the tribe living in the vicinity of Québec, had forced him however to reconsider his assumptions and expectations of both the land, and its people. Even if he didn't understand them, he had come to admire much about the native people. And he admits now, to himself, that his efforts to convert them to Christianity have only weakened and confused them. This has been his most bitter realization and personal trial. At times, it plagues him and shakes his convictions to their core.

What is he really doing here? Who and what, in the end, is he serving?

Before him now, yet one more time, sits another new agent sent by Cardinal Richelieu to hurry things along. Champlain has not been with him five minutes and already he detests the man. Father du Barre, the new Jesuit superior assigned to New France, arrived a day ago on the supply ships.

He can already see that du Barre, with his naive, misguided enthusiasm, will lord the rigid structures of his Catholic convictions over the Algonquin and Québec and smother the colony, until…well, until what?

Champlain pulls his gaze from the view out the window, back to the du Barre sitting across from him, to the priest's thin white face, carefully cropped black beard and the meticulous elegance of his black robe. Slowly and repeatedly turning the finely crafted silver and ivory crucifix in his hand, he exudes a confident impenetrability, alerting Champlain to what he knows will be impractical and time-consuming nonsense.

Du Barre, ever so piously and humbly, has been taking pains to describe his position in court and most importantly, his relationship to Cardinal Richelieu. Despite himself, Champlain's attention has drifted off. A sudden silence draws him back; du Barre has stopped speaking. Champlain scrutinizes the priest, and suddenly realizes who this man reminds him of, in fact who he models himself after: Father Joseph, l'Eminence Grise, that terrifyingly powerful and ruthless Capuchin monk, advisor to Richelieu. He also realizes he has offended the man and if he is anything like Father Joseph, he must be careful. He knows he has inadvertently created tension between them and must now work to bridge it.

"Sorry, Father du Barre. So why has the good Cardinal sent you here?"

"I was saying, His Eminence does not wish to lose New France again."

"We received no supply ships for over two years. We were a week away from starvation. All of us."

Nothing makes Champlain as angry as the insinuation that somehow he had lost New France while France had been at war with England. France had in fact abandoned Québec, desperately overextended on the home front. And the English had simply seized the opportunity. With no supplies or munitions from France for over two years, Champlain had been forced to surrender. When the war ended later that same year, New France was returned by treaty. Yet even now, Richelieu continues to blame Champlain. Du Barre dismisses Champlain's agitation with a regal turn of his hand.

"The English are pushing further north and west from their colonies—"

"As I have been reporting for years."

Du Barre eyes Champlain sharply, then continues, "— and Cardinal Richelieu wishes to create a new colony strategic to keeping the flow of furs to France for the long term. A new colony east of here, well-fortified, to stop this move of the English north. "

"The English have created an uneasy alliance with the Iroquois," says Champlian. "I strongly recommended several years ago, in one of my several reports, that it would be strategically wise to build a second colony at Trois-Rivières with a well-garrisoned fort between us at Ile Saint Croix. We could defend a colony there, and the growing season is longer — another advantage."

The priest continues as though Champlain hasn't spoken. "In exchange for all trading rights in New France, the new Company of One Hundred Associates has agreed to fund four thousand settlers over fifteen years. Three hundred a year. Each new colonist will be sponsored for three years."

Champlain raises his eyes in disbelief at the audacity of these numbers — three hundred a year! It's hopelessly unrealistic. But he is careful to watch his words, choosing to reply with one simple fact so he doesn't appear to be over-reacting and offend the priest yet further.

"We have been here twenty-five years and do not yet have two hundred settlers in Québec."

"You can be sure His Eminence is aware of your success here," du Barre responds.

Champlain can feel his cheeks burning at the priest's implied rebuke. After trying for so long to gain support for New France, to convince the court of the colony's value, this was indeed glorious news. It is in fact a vindication of his years of fostering and promotion. But the way in which du Barre delivers the news infuriates him. He stares at the priest, speechless. If the man stays, what, he wonders, if anything, would strip him of this pious superiority? Where is the chink in his formidable armour? He had seen this land strip men bare over and over again and without much mercy.

Du Barre continues. "Cardinal Richelieu is making a huge financial commitment to this. In return, he will need to see real profits, returned to France, not only to Québec. We would expand the fur trade. We believe we can find gold and silver here much as the Spanish have found to the south. And we will look for a route to the Indies."

Champlain holds up his hand and opens his mouth to reply, then slumps back in his chair. France, yet again, has sent another emissary of futility.

"You propose a fantasy. We have never found gold or silver. Nor have the natives or they would have brought it to us because they know we look for it. And there is no route to the Indies."

"The land cannot go on forever."

"Perhaps, but you travel this land in canoes, not trading ships. We know what lies over a thousand miles west of here and from the reports of the tribes there, what lies another five hundred miles west of that."

Du Barre's eyes narrow. "How do you know that?" Champlain hesitates, anticipating exactly what du Barre will bring up next.

"This Brulé," du Barre almost spits out the name, and Champlain sags a little more in his chair realizing just how predictably this conversation will unfold. "Do you truly believe this trade arrangement you have with him for furs best serves the interests of France?"

"With all due respect Father du Barre, Brulé is the fur trade. He has lived out there with the Wendat for twenty-five years. As long as I have been here. All the trade routes to the north and the west for hundreds of miles, he has created those. He has created the relationships with all the tribes, speaks their languages and dialects. All that trade funnels through the Wendat and then to us. Because of him. Because of Brulé."

"A useful foundation to be sure——"

"He will not help you."

"What do you mean he will not help me. As of now he works for me." The absurdity of the idea causes Champlain to snort, despite himself.

"What is so amusing?" The priest, accustomed to members of the

French court humbling themselves in his presence, fumes at what he sees as Champlain's impertinence.

Again, Champlain realizes he has offended du Barre. His sense of diplomacy is normally innate, automatic; he reads people easily. But looking at du Barre now, Champlain realizes he cannot fathom what lies beneath the priest's arrogant, pious exterior. Except that he doesn't like it. Or trust it.

He responds as patiently as he can, "We have a simple arrangement. We stay out of the Land of the Wendat. Brulé brings the furs. That supports Québec. And that supports France."

"We do not need to honor this dismal agreement if we plan to colonize there."

"Where? You mean in the Land of the Wendat?"

Du Barre nods. "We must claim this territory for France. Now, before the English push further north. Not just on paper, but with colonies."

In all the years Champlain has been governor in Québec, listening to the latest schemes and plans for the New World arriving fresh from the French court, nothing has come close to this in utter outrageousness. He turns away from the penetrating glare of the priest and again gazes out the window to avoid saying or doing something he might regret. The two men he had seen smoking earlier have disappeared. He collects himself and then states, in as even a voice as he can muster, "That is ridiculous."

"My dear Monsieur Champlain, you sent a report yourself to this effect. Your exploration from what, twenty years ago? You see, we do read your reports. Based on your description we thought it an excellent location for a colony."

"I think what I wrote was, yes, the area around Ossossane in the Land of the Wendat would make a good colony. But, first, we would need to build four or five well-garrisoned forts linking Quebéc and Ossossane together."

"We have sufficient numbers and resources now…and I think you underestimate the ability of our troops."

Champlain pounds his fist on the desk. Rising abruptly, he knocks his chair out of the way and turns to jab his finger at a large map hanging on the wall.

"We are here." He jabs again. "The Wendat live there. That is five hundred miles of savage, relentless wilderness infested with Iroquois. The only safe route to the Land of the Wendat is a north route of over eight hundred miles. You cannot build a colony there. Not a colony of five hundred. Not a colony of fifty. You cannot possibly imagine the difficulty of what you propose. Unless, you go there yourself. Then you would see. Then you would understand that what you say is a fantasy."

"That is exactly what I have been sent here to do."

"What?"

"To see the Land of the Wendat for myself."

"You are mad!"

"You have been there."

Champlain looks at the priest, sizing up just how long this man would last in a wilderness as unrelenting and unforgiving as that which lies to the west, which the priest so arrogantly hoped to conquer. Du Barre feels the scrutiny.

"I take with me the will of the Crown of France."

"It will not be the will of the Crown out there with you, Father. Out there, in the wilderness, it will be your will and yours alone."

33

Four days later, Petashwa sorts through the expedition supplies strewn out along the loading dock by the river below Québec. His attention shifts from the three oversized trunks perched on the dock, to the slow descent of their owners down the steep hill from the fort and to several finely-crafted Algonquin birch bark canoes. The canoes measure twenty and twenty-two feet. The trunks belong in the hold of a ship, not in a canoe.

Father du Barre arrives on the dock, ignoring Petashwa and the three Algonquin assisting him. He looks over the supplies as the rest of the French party now join him. Two are French nobles, the Marquis Joseph-Albert de Clemont and the Count Jean-Marie de Valery.

To Petashwa, the nobles resemble rare exotic birds, attired in their high-heeled, buckled shoes, silk stockings, brocade frock coats with their huge cuffs of silk and lace. They sport finely groomed beards, long, elaborate wigs with oversized black hats aloft with plumage. Each lean on tall, silver-handled walking sticks and, hanging at their waists, fine, jewelled ornamental swords. Neither man can be older than thirty. Two well-dressed servants hover behind them.

"Father du Barre, we cannot have finished this discussion," complains the Marquis, mopping his face with a lace handkerchief. "He has no idea what it is like here. He thinks Québec is a town."

The Count de Valery scoffs. "A few wooden sheds. It is bestial. And look at that," waving his hand out across the river, assuming the gesture at the wilderness speaks for itself.

Du Barre looks at them severely. "Cardinal Richelieu made it very clear."

"But he had no idea—"

"I think in fact, he did," corrected du Barre. "Your parents pleaded for you. You should count yourselves lucky. It could have been much worse."

"Than this?" De Clemont looks down, chastened and angry.

While they thoroughly ignore Petashwa, he studiously watches them. The two nobles seem like children — de Clemont mean and destructive; de Valery, weak and looking to de Clemont for direction. The priest he fears immediately, intuitively; something about him does not match the smooth exterior he presents. What lies beneath that exterior Petashwa cannot read but it feels neither simple nor kind — two qualities every other priest in Québec at least aspires to.

Petashwa was wary of priests in the past but over the years, as his responsibilities grew and the relationship with Champlain became more open and intimate, Champlain had exerted more pressure on him to convert to Christianity. And in the end he did. In name at least. But in truth, as he became more enmeshed with the French in Québec, and hence had to make some show of his interest in Christianity, he found in fact, he was bewildered by it. Bewildered by how distant and different the Christian God was to his own idea of a Great Spirit that was present and alive everywhere he looked…at least when he was in the woods and not in the boxed confines of the fort.

He did not understand the reasons for worshipping this man Jesus or why he was so important to the Christians. Nor could he understand why anyone would live under the constant threat of hellfire and damnation. Forever. He knew when he posed questions to the priests they found him simple-minded. Most of the priests treated him and the other

Algonquin like children. But not Champlain. Champlain had struggled with the Algonquin language and still tried to learn it. But he sized up each Algonquin individually, clearly and, to Petashwa's mind, fairly. Champlain trusted him now. So when he told Champlain about these three trunks, their size, their weight, it had led to this. Now the three Frenchmen are here and Petashwa wonders how to start and what to say.

"Who are we supposed to speak to?" asks de Clemont. "We've come all the way down here in this heat and there is no one here."

"You come to talk with me," Petashwa responds in French.

De Clemont turns his head abruptly at these words and notices Petashwa for the first time.

"You?"

"Yes, sir."

"This is Champlain's assistant," explains du Barre.

"A savage?" says de Clemont.

Champlain had warned Petashwa how they might react. "I will be your guide."

"Really? You must jest," says de Clemont turning to du Barre perplexed.

"Sir, I have been to the Land of the Wendat many times," Petashwa says.

"Champlain assures me that if anyone can get us there and back alive, it will be this one," adds du Barre.

Both de Clemont and de Valery exclaim, "Alive? What do you mean alive?"

Petashwa knows that Champlain had made repeated efforts, in vain, to explain to du Barre the dangers of taking the shorter of the two routes to the Land of the Wendat. He'd repeated the warnings of the Wendat traders from earlier in the summer that the Iroquois were out and active on that route. But the priest had ignored Champlain's warnings, "I have my soldiers, They are French, fresh, well-disciplined," he insisted, "and more than able to handle any threat these Iroquois may pose."

Petashwa knew the soldiers' European training in warfare would prove useless against the Iroquois. But he said nothing. Instead Petashwa says, "Sirs, if I may, I speak to you about what you bring on this exploration," pointing at the trunks.

"We had our trunks brought this morning, just as we were instructed," answers de Clemont.

"We packed the bare minimum as we were told," added de Valery.

"Sirs, we are traveling in those canoes." Petashwa now points at the seven birch bark canoes lying at the end of the dock. Five men in each."

"In those?" scoffs de Clemont. "That is ridiculous."

"Thirty-five of us with all our belongings for two months," clarifies Petashwa.

Something of what lies ahead begins to form in de Clemont's mind for the first time.

"I left the most opulent court in Europe, for this. I am at least going to be comfortable. I can not take less," snaps de Clemont.

Du Barre surveys the trunks, one of them his, and the size of the canoes. He admires his piety and is more than willing to suffer for Christ, or the Crown, if need be. "Yes, I see," he says. "Can you supply me with a smaller case? Monsieurs de Clemont and de Valery, you will cut your belongings in half and repack them in cases which I am sure these…men will be happy to supply you with."

"Half!"

"And just one servant for the two of you. Is that correct?" looking at Petashwa.

"One?" they both whined. "But whose. I can't leave without —"

Du Barre raises his hand to silence them. "I am sure you can come to some agreement."

It is clear to Petashwa that du Barre takes pleasure in adding to the nobles' misery. He feels he needs to add one more thing. "Sirs, I fear you will have difficulty traveling dressed like that. We can supply —"

De Clemont turns on him, "We represent the Court of Louis the XIII. And we will continue to represent the court even here."

Beside a river, meandering through a wide expanse of open land, surrounded by forest, stands Ossossane, a Wendat village. A palisade, a sturdy twenty-foot wall, several layers thick, of sharpened pine poles, surrounds and protects the village. Stretching away from the village and the river into the heat-hazed distance, Wendat tend their ripening crops of corn, beans and squash.

Two hundred yards from the palisade, isolated and forlorn on the far side of the corn and squash crops, hugging the edge of the forest, sits a rough hut of bark. A large, wooden cross made of two stripped pine logs stands before its entrance and a tarnished bell hangs next to the doorway. Above the door hangs a now weather-beaten crucifix. Whether by intention or chance, the eyes of Christ gaze directly out at the palisade wall of the Wendat village.

Inside the small chapel several logs serve as pews on the dirt floor. But the bark hut is empty now save for two priests who kneel in front of the wooden altar. A candle burning in its silver holder and a silver cross standing on an altar cloth almost transform the lowly space. The priests say Mass.

Not a mile away, and much deeper into the forest, another bark hut nestles in isolation. Inside, alone, the Wendat shaman Okatwan, chants. He chants a slow, rhythmic cry, more animal than human, as he beats a hide drum. Firelight flickers in his luminous eyes. He stares, as if transfixed, as if seeing something not of this world, but another. Mingled with his voice, mirroring its rhythm, other voices around him seem to pulse and reverberate in accompaniment.

Back in the small chapel, the two priests finish their Mass, but continue to kneel, savouring the silence and solace of the service. Father LeCharon, pale, bearded and gaunt, takes a deep breath and lifts his head. He rises slowly, stiff from kneeling for so long. Father Marquette, red beard and complexion, gazes up at the altar and crosses himself. Both dress in threadbare, patched black robes. The black robes of the Jesuits.

Father Marquette now stands, tall, straight and confident. Father LeCharon glances uneasily at him, but Marquette has already turned and started for the door, so he follows. They walk in silence through shafts of sunlight filtering through the cracks in the bark roof. The light glows through the incense smoke. LeCharon looks at the empty pews.

When they first arrived here the Wendat had sent them a dozen boys for instruction. Now he realizes the Wendat had just been polite, hospitable. The boys were wild and undisciplined and so Father Marquette had brandished a stick to try and gain some order. Eventually, in his frustration, he used it and the boys scattered and ran out the door with him chasing behind them. They were the last Wendat to enter the chapel. That was almost eight months ago.

Marquette dips his fingers in a small wooden bowl of water set by the door, crosses himself again, pulls aside the oil cloth that serves as the makeshift door and walks outside, shielding his piercing blue eyes from the harsh sunlight. LeCharon stands, squinting beside him. Both look at the palisade of the Wendat village. LeCharon, unaware he has let out a long sigh, feels his shoulders sag. The spiritual solace and lift from Mass dissipates in the breeze.

A loud banging jolts them both to attention. Marquette turns, grabs a stick leaning against the wall and strides around the side of the chapel. A group of Wendat boys, practically naked, bang on the side of the bark wall of the hut with sticks, shouting. Marquette races towards them, the stick raised ready to strike, reenacting once again his futile attempt at discipline. The boys scream and run, taunting Marquette, as they disappear into the safety of the forest. LeCharon follows more slowly. As the last boy slips out of sight he surveys the dense wall of trees in front of him. "What a grim exile." Marquette frowns and turns his fanatical gaze upon LeCharon, "In the eyes of Our Lord, Jean-Philippe, the greater the test, the greater the glory."

The four canoes of the Wendat rise and fall on the slow swell of a seemingly limitless lake, called by the Wendat, Attiguautan.* Its offing unfolds into water and sky as endless as an ocean. Paddling south, the canoes hug the shoreline of smooth, pink granite islands lapped incessantly by the waves of crystal clear water. Sculpted pine trees, twisted and bent by the prevailing west wind, claw for existence through the stone. When first travelling here with Brulé more than twenty years earlier, Champlain had called it "la mer douce", or the sweet sea, both because it wasn't salt water, but also because of its vast, rugged beauty.

Now, after a month of travelling, they are almost home. With each stroke their hands brush the cold water as the waves lap and drum the sides of the canoe. Brulé has always savoured these fur trading expeditions. In the long hours of paddling out on the lake, his mind slowly empties out, becomes quiet, open, at peace, as if the peace and spirit of the land were somehow finding resonance within him and flowing through him. He feels connected, enlarged and comforted by a force for which he has no words. Champlain had always encouraged, almost begged him, to keep journals, make notes and take compass readings to help map the vast unknown wilderness he had come to know so well. But Brulé found the longer he settled into the world of the Wendat, the less was his desire or need to write.

The greater desire was to let go, embrace the deep sense of attunement

*Georgian Bay

with the natural unfolding of events, ebbing and flowing, playing out and dispersing, moment by moment, around him. He navigates, now, to a different compass.

But something has changed, and that peace feels shattered. Since the gruesome discovery of the murdered tribesmen a week ago, he cannot avoid a mounting sense of dread. The Iroquois represent the Wendat's most fearsome enemy. At this point on the journey, so close to home, his companions would normally be joking and laughing amongst themselves. Instead, they are sullen, withdrawn. He senses their unease, as if something has shifted in their world that they cannot yet understand. Brulé though, understands only too well. He had seen how in Québec the Algonquin and the Wendat lusted after muskets and had never traded the Wendat furs for them. The Jesuits had seen it too, and knew that desire was all they might have to convince the Wendat to embrace Christianity. The irony of that never escaped Brulé — guns for Christ. He had never brought one back to the Wendat. But now…

They have pushed hard to get home, paddling from sunrise to sunset. Usually so at peace in the woods, Brulé is impatient now to reach Ossossane, their village, to see his wife, ensure the village is safe, and to talk with Atironta, the Wendat chief.

They paddle east past several islands and around a long arm of smooth rock. Beyond, the land transforms dramatically into forest and open meadows.

"I've been agonizing over what we'll find at the village," says Brulé.

"We will know now soon enough," says Savignon. "These Iroquois guns…you know I always hated the raids and the skirmishes we had with the Iroquois. I just lost my taste for proving myself like that in France.

Lost courage maybe. I could not strut, chest puffed and be counted as a warrior, for my people. But this is different. It pushes the problem right into our face, right into the safety of our villages."

"I don't think it is courage you lack, Savignon. But I understand." Brulé was prodably the only one who did understand. Many Wendat found Savignon a bit strange and aloof since his return so many years ago. His French experience formed him in the very years he would have become a warrior at home. But Brulé found much in him to admire and the two have been fast friends for over twenty years.

They continue for several more miles up a slow-moving river until, finally, their village comes into view. Relief floods through Brulé. No disaster has struck. The village looks unchanged. Smoke from cook fires drifts peacefully from the many longhouses behind the palisade. Children and dogs run and play outside the village. Men and women are busy harvesting the beans in the fields.

They slide into shore, store the bark canoes carefully, shoulder their bales of furs, and head up to the village. Children run excitedly to greet them. Those in the fields wave as they pass. The small Chippawa boy clings to Brulé's hand. Together they make their way from the river up to the palisade and the entrance to the village.

Inside a longhouse, a Wendat woman in her thirties carefully tends to a young girl lying close to the heat of the cook fire. The girl, gripped by fever, shivers and glistens with sweat. She is weak, angry boils cover most of her arms and face. A young boy bursts into the longhouse and rushes up to the woman, "They are here."

The woman is Kinta, Brulé's wife. She smiles, places a cool cloth on the girl's forehead and wipes her hands on some damp moss by the fire.

Her step, though not rushed, reveals her keenness to see her husband after so many weeks apart. Leaving the longhouse she makes her way to the entrance of the village. There is no gate, but rather a twisting passage through the palisade poles so narrow that only one person can pass at a time. Villagers congregate at the entrance.

As the travellers move through the opening, they are greeted warmly by their families. Brulé sees Kinta and embraces her. She immediately notices the boy and then the bandages. She kneels, touching the dressing. "What happened to him? Who is he?"

"He was shot," Brulé says.

That word, "shot", quickly spreads through the crowd. Everyone begins talking, wanting details, wanting to understand how this could have happened. "Who did this?" asks Kinta.

Brulé knows his answer is not what they want to hear. "Iroquois."

The crowd momentarily goes silent, in a shock of fear and confusion, before erupting into a frenzy of further questions. Brulé kneels quickly beside his wife, "Look after him, Kinta, I must meet with Atironta." He then pushes his way through the crowd and the questions and heads through the village to the chief's longhouse.

Atironta, the Wendat chief, sits, his bearing as regal as any king. He puffs on his long pipe. "How many guns could the Iroquois have?" he asks after listening patiently but with growing alarm to Brulé's recounting of the killings.

"I have no idea," answers Brulé, "but we must find out. We might fight against ten. But not thirty."

"Your Champlain has not allowed us to have guns."

"It is the black robes, not Champlain. Champlain will hate this almost as much as we do. Believe me, this is not good news for him. But he will always do what he must for Québec. Atironta, you must understand something. Until now, you know, our war with the Iroquois has not been about killing. Yes, two or three die each year. Prisoners get taken, both Wendat and Iroquois. But men fight for valor. We honor the skill of war, not death. What you must understand is that guns change that.

"With twenty or thirty guns, maybe twenty or thirty Wendat will die. If we have guns in our hands we will seek revenge and twenty or thirty Iroquois will die. And it will not stop there. They will then come and do the same again to us. The need for revenge will grip us and control us. And each year we will use our furs to trade for more guns. And more will die. More Wendat. More Iroquois. This is the warfare of the white man … and I tell you, it will destroy us."

Atironta pulls long and silently on his pipe. Smoke drifts and curls around him as he ponders Brulé's words. "White Hawk, what you say may be true. My people have made me chief because they know I will do everything to lead them well, and wisely. I am Wendat. I have no faith in Iroquois. If they have guns, we need guns."

"If we go down this path, it will consume us. Both Wendat and Iroquois." Then Brulé ventures to suggest the idea he has been turning over and over in his mind since they found those dead warriors strewn on the beach. "Perhaps the Iroquois could understand that they play into the hands of the English and their schemes. Perhaps they will understand that this is all bound to ruin them as surely as it will ruin us."

"Who can make an Iroquois understand that?" asks Atironta.

"What of Siskwa," answered Brulé, "the Iroquois chief. If you could talk —"

Atironta shakes his head. "Talk?"

"We have done it before. Once or twice, to buy back a captured chief."

The chief waves the suggestion away. "Yes, an exchange." They fall silent, each lost in thought, until Brulé once again tries to urge his idea upon Atironta. "I grew up with the endless, merciless killing of the white man's wars. My own father fought and died in one of those wars. When I left France, I sought to rid myself of the stupidity and misery of it all. I left it behind me and vowed that I would never see such senseless killing here."

"You may have vowed that in the past," says Atironta, "but what do we do now? I cannot talk to Siskwa. He knows the French do not trade with us for guns. He will not see the danger you speak of. He will only see that I come with nothing to trade but my fear."

Brulé lowers his head and stares at the embers of the fire between himself and Atironta. The turmoil he had been feeling since discovering the dozen dead men now returns in full force. The inevitability of the idea that had presented itself to him returned now and made his stomach turn.

He knew all along Atironta would not, could not, talk to Siskwa, or truly see what confronted the Wendat. Only he had seen the kind of bloodshed this could lead to, and what lay ahead for them now if guns replaced arrows and tomahawks as weapons. Only he had seen how many people die in the ugliness of mechanized warfare. And only he had seen how the finances to purchase those guns would consume them. Once one warrior holds a gun in his hand, every warrior will want one. The picture of ruin unfolds like a lurid nightmare before his eyes, as he gazes at the dying embers. Everything he loved about the Wendat and their way of life — the life he now considered his own — would wither and die. He could not let that happen. He tries again.

"Then perhaps I can be the one to speak for the Wendat. I have heard of Siskwa's wisdom. Perhaps he will understand. I cannot stand by and do nothing. I cannot watch our lives be overtaken with the kind of slaughter I have witnessed in my own country. I cannot do that."

"You are a warrior. I have fought beside you. I have not seen what you say of the white man's war. I only know my own people's war with the Iroquois. I see this as something I may not fully understand. But I remember what happened on your last visit to the Iroquois. I fear the only thing you will gain this time is your own death, bound to an Iroquois torture stake."

The sounds of chopping wood echo through the camp and out over the lake. Each evening, immediately upon landing, a dozen French soldiers begin the repeated but necessary task of cutting down saplings to construct their fortified palisade. They must choose a campsite either on an island where there is less need of the palisade or on a long arm of land jutting out into the lake or river. The sturdy palisade across the narrow point of land helps diminish the possibility of attack from the forest behind them; they can spot anyone approaching from the water well in advance.

The others in the group, Algonquin and French aides, unload the canoes, gather wood and kindling for the fires and begin to prepare food. Somewhat apart from the bustle of activity, rest two small wooden tables. Champlain sits, working at one. At the other sit the two magnificently dressed French noblemen, attended by a single footman. Champlain stares over at the incongruous image before him: candlelight flickers and dances over the nobles' table, over the damask table cloth, over the crystal decanters, silver cups and porcelain plates, in what seems a willful defiance of the reality of the wilderness.

De Valery stares out across the river. Evening light gilds the hilltops on the far side of the water, their pale orange shimmers against the deep purple of the shoreline. Bored, de Clement taps his fingers impatiently on the table and gazes about at the activity. He looks over at Champlain.

De Clemont turns to the footman, "Tell Monsieur Champlain we would like to talk to him." He adds, "I am sure he can amuse us."

De Valery, curious what Champlain is doing at his desk, says, "I will get him." As he approaches, Champlain stops writing and stands, "Monsieur le Count, what an honor." He wonders how long, in this forested wilderness, such court protocol will last.

"The Marquis de Clemont asked that you join us, but I am interested to know what you are working on. What do you have there?"

Champlain turns the map towards de Valery. It is covered in calculations and measurements. "I made a map twenty years ago when I last visited the Wendat. I am checking and verifying my measurements. We have claimed the territory for France. We should at least know what it is we control."

De Valery runs his finger over the map to the vague contours of the territory's western edge. Champlain sighs, "Completely unknown. At least to me."

"Come join us for a glass of wine." Obliged by a sense of protocol, Champlain accepts, despite his reservations.

He picks up his chair and walks over to join the nobles at their lavishly laden table. The footman offers him a glass of wine. De Clemont notices a smudge of dirt on his stocking and brushes at it, annoyed. He mops his forehead with a lace handkerchief. Both nobles have that affected, effeminate court manner that had always annoyed Champlain when in the French Court.

"Each evening you build this wall," comments de Valery.

"Palisade, Monsieur le Count. You must always fortify your camp."

"I can only imagine what breathes just beyond that wall in the dark of night," says de Clemont. "But we never see anyone."

"That actually worries me," muses Champlain. "Normally we would encounter Algonquin fishing camps from time to time."

"Worries you? Why does that worry you?" asks de Clemont, slightly unnerved by the statement.

Champlain waves the question away, not wanting to alarm them with tales of the Iroquois. He takes a sip of wine and casually looks out at the camp in a manner that he hopes will change the topic.

"Tell me, Monsieur Champlain. Why did you come? I have wanted to ask, but never felt it was the correct moment. As for us, the Marquis and I did not exactly choose this," confesses de Valery.

Champlain gazes over at du Barre busy directing affairs on the other side of the clearing. "He said he would have me sent back to France in irons if I didn't. I think the good Cardinal wanted it. As punishment likely…for something."

"Yes, punishment," muses de Clemont. "Du Barre has a way about him, doesn't he? Pulls you in with his charm."

"I asked him," said de Valery, "about this fellow Brulé."

"Ah, yes, Brulé drives the Jesuits mad," answers Champlain, barely disguising the subtle pleasure he derives from the effect Brulé has on the priest.

"But not you?" asks de Valery.

"No, not me," answers Champlain. "Brulé created the fur trade with us. And the fur trade supports Québec. I am more practical than pious."

"This fur trade is so…so unexpected now that we are here," de Valery remarks, as he takes off his large, stylish black hat and looks at it. "We wear these hats at home. We are assured they are real beaver. That nothing less will ever do. If you had asked me I could have told you that the hat is made from the pelt of a beaver. But I never gave any thought to the idea someone had to actually find a beaver out here and kill it. The man just comes to court with the new hat samples and you buy one."

"And you need at least one new hat each season," adds de Clemont.

"We send out hundreds of pelts every year. All of them through the Wendat," Champlain tells them.

"In Québec they told us this Brulé has made a fortune with this monopoly of his on the furs. Is this true?" queries de Clemont.

"The arrangement is simple. He brings the furs to Québec each year and no one else is allowed into the interior. He wants to keep the disease and alcohol out. And the church. That is his goal, his motivation. And I understand why. He saw what all three did to the Algonquin in

50

Québec." Champlain stares out across the river for a moment. "I think it is my deepest regret, how we have served, or rather not served, the Algonquin. The Jesuits in Québec always push to send missionaries out to the Wendat. We finally sent two last year. That was a heated issue with Brulé I can tell you. He split my desk with his tomahawk."

"But what does he do with the money?" asks de Valery.

"I have no idea," answers Champlain, "Obviously, he cannot spend it out here."

"Perhaps he will retire to France one day?"

Champlain shakes his head. "He hates being in Québec for more than three or four days. I cannot imagine he will ever return to France. He will die here, I imagine. As will I."

The forest grows thick and abundant around them, as Kinta follows Brulé along the well-trodden path. Oaks, maples and pines stand like giant sentinels, some four feet in width, their canopy a huge shaded arc a hundred feet about the forest floor. At this time of day, bird song fills the air, a jay screeches. Animals bolt in the underbrush. A red squirrel chatters above them.

They walk, listening to the forest sounds, glad to once again be together. A tall, granite cliff appears ahead through the trees, its entire surface is etched in markings — a carved tapestry of petroglyphs: men and animals, suns and moons, boats and fish, and strange indecipherable symbols. Some are ancient, the carved lines as weathered and dark as the rock face itself. Others, more recent, stand out like pale scars. Brulé runs his hand over the surface, tracing his finger into the carved grooves. He loves the sense of power, the deep and tangible connection to the spirit of nature he feels here in the presence of the petroglyphs. He takes tobacco from the pouch hanging from his belt and carefully pushes leaves into a long vertical crack in the rock face, as he recites a Wendat incantation. He hands some tobacco to Kinta who repeats an incantation of her own.

From the rock wall, in a clearing through the trees, Brulé spots Okatwan, the Wendat shaman. The man is naked but for a breechcloth and a headdress of wood and feathers that has been carved into the shape of a long beak. A dense tangle of strands hang from his neck — claws, shells, fur, amulets, and small pouches made of hide. His chest and arms are marked with swirling designs of black and yellow paint.

Okatwan sits, completely still, several feet away from a wolf in the clearing. They face one another, eyes locked. Brulé can feel the current of energy and connection flowing in the space between the two.

Suddenly the spell is broken. Okatwan feels Brulé's presence, turns to meet his gaze and in that instant, Brulé realizes the wolf is gone. Vanished.

Okatwan motions and Brulé and Kinta follow him silently to his lodging. As their eyes adjust to the dim light of the interior, a dense alchemy of shamanic medicine slowly emerges. Pots and jars filled with dark liquids and pastes line the permeter of the hut. Skulls, bones, herbs and plants hang from the roof. Their murky odour mixes with the fragrance of the wood smoke from the fire. On a nearby perch sits a raven, its black eyes alert, watching them. The three sit in silence for some time before Okatwan shakes his head and speaks. "I can find no medicine that speaks to this disease. Nor will it speak to me. I have travelled far into the spirit world to understand this thing, but it comes from a place I do not know and I cannot enter. I have no understanding or power over it."

"I have seen with my own eyes how many of the Algonquin died because of this same disease," Brulé tells him.

"It is only now, after the black robes come to us, that the people become sick," adds Kinta.

Okatwan nods. "I have seen only one thing, but this one thing spoke to me clearly. You must get the sick out of the village, away from the others. Build huts for them. Care for them there. If you do as I say, we can stop this disease. For now. Perhaps for many seasons. Perhaps it will not then come back. But you must do it now. You must not wait."

Back in the village, Kinta ladles stew from a large iron pot over the fire into a wooden bowl and hands it to Brulé. The small Chippawa boy snuggles close to her, staring into the fire. She strokes his hair tenderly; he attaches himself to her more and more, accepting her affection. They look up suddenly as Atsan, Brulé's son, walks into the longhouse. Atsan is eighteen, with a strong physique and handsome features. He looks Wendat, but for the clear blue eyes he has inherited from his father. As he sits down next to them at the fire, Kinta hands him a bowl of the steaming stew. But as he reaches for it, Brulé notices three stripes of blood wiped onto his son's arm.

"So he prepares you all for battle, firing your courage, puffing up your chests," taunts Brulé.

"Tonda is our war chief. That is what he does."

"He will get you all killed, Atsan."

"I am Wendat. I crave to prove myself against the Iroquois. That is our Wendat honor. To fight the enemy"

"What you face now are Iroquois bullets. There is no honor or valor in a bullet. The Iroquois did not even scalp their kill. They were ashamed I think, at what they had done. Tonda does not yet understand it, but he will the first time he encounters what the guns do."

"What would you have us do then? Hide?"

"If we have guns, who do you think will win? You think maybe the Wendat. Or the Iroquois. But you would be wrong. Neither of us will win. It will be the French who win. And the English."

"You trade with the French for us. You cannot just say we cannot fight bullets and then do nothing. We cannot do nothing. We must get guns also."

"Atsan, you speak without knowledge. You speak without experience. You cannot imagine this warfare of guns until you have seen a thousand dead on a battlefield. Imagine all the Wendat and all the Iroquois combined, ten times that number died in the wars of Europe when I was young. My father fought in those wars in France. He died in those wars. Death for God. Death for Wendat honor. It makes no difference. Fight the Iroquois with guns once and you will know you must have one. My fear is that the guns will be the end of the Wendat, and the Iroquois." Brulé nods at the three stripes of blood on Atsan's arm. "This, this glorifying of valour and honour, with guns? That will destroy us."

"Well then, what would you do?" Atsan scoffs. "I suppose you would just send a party of Wendat to smoke the peace pipe with the Iroquois. I suppose that is your solution."

"In fact, that is my solution. That is what I am going to do," answers Brulé.

Atsan jolts back in alarm, stunned at his father's response. "To the Iroquois? You are going to make peace with our enemy? You think they will listen? To you!" He glares at Brulé in a fury of confusion. Brulé holds his son's look, then lowers his head. "I don't know, Atsan. Perhaps I put too much trust in what I have heard of Siskwa. He has done much to unite the Iroquois and create harmony among their tribes. Atironta is a great chief but he cannot yet see what harm, what damage, these guns will do. Who but me has seen it? I stand in the middle of all this and I must act, speak for the Wendat, whether I like it or not."

Atsan stands, at a loss for words. Just then, Savignon enters the longhouse. Atsan, not wanting to deal with this any further in front of him, turns abruptly and leaves. Brulé watches his son depart and then turns to Savignon, "I have never seen a storm as black as the one coming to us now."

"Well, while you speak of a black storm, I have just spoken with Marquette, the priest. He scares me that man. Because I am the only Wendat who he can communicate with, I feel he grips me with talons. His eyes burn into me when he speaks. But he wants to talk to you."

"They have brought disease to our village and then they tell us they want to save us," says Brulé. "You can tell them to go to hell."

"I am sure they feel they arrived in hell a year ago when they first came here and have just been sinking deeper since. They reminded me, and asked me to tell you, that you promised to help them learn the Wendat language. You did say, you would help them when you got back this time.

They wanted me to remind you, you said the same thing last time and you did not. Their point is they can do nothing if they cannot speak to the villagers and they want me to remind you again that they have been here a year."

"But you have helped them learn Wendat."

"I have tried. But they only focus on the words they need like kingdom, lord, saviour. I can't find a Wendat word for it and need ten, and then they can't begin to understand what I am getting at. They suspect it is my fault, that I am too simple-minded. They think you will explain it better."

"They think the Wendat are stupid and simple. So they think the language of such a simple people must be simple. They hammer at it with their Jesuit reason and get nowhere." He looks at Savignon a moment, forgetting about the priests, then asks. "You think my going is foolish don't you?"

Savignon cocks his head to one side, "Etienne, I remember what came stumbling out of the forest the last time you visited the Iroquois."

Brulé grimaces at the thought. He looks over at Kinta who has pulled the Chippawa boy onto her lap, holding him tight against her. Brulé strokes her hair. Their eyes lock, each knowing without words the other's thoughts and feeling the direction destiny seems to be pulling each of them.

As Brulé leaves the longhouse with Savignon, they find Atsan lingering by the doorway. He joins them as they head through the village. Brulé can see his son is agitated and wanting to say something. Finally he blurts out, "What am I supposed to think? I am Wendat, raised to fight Iroquois. I have to constantly prove myself because you are white. They need to see if it is white beneath my skin. And now you want to go and talk to them and —"

Atsan suddenly falls silent as they approach the longhouse of Tonda, the Wendat war chief. Tonda is the last person Atsan wants to have witness his confusion. The chief sits on the ground sharpening a tomahawk. He has a formidable, aggressive presence. Atsan stops in front of him. Tonda looks up.

"Tonda, what do you think of this?" asks Atsan, "White Hawk feels we cannot fight against the guns of the Iroquois."

Though Tonda admires Brulé — the white man has proven himself many times in battle — he feels compelled to dismiss his concern. "I do not fear Iroquois. With guns or without guns."

Atsan continues, "He says we must go and talk with them." At this, Tonda looks sharply up at Brulé. "He says the guns will destroy us all. He goes to talk with the Iroquois, with Siskwa. Will you go with him?"

As Atsan speaks these words, despite himself, a shadow of fear passes over Tonda's powerful face. "I have spoken with Iroquois. I have spoken with Siskwa. But always we had something they wanted. You cannot go like this, with an empty basket." His fear quickly turns to anger. "I know how to fight Iroquois," he says, "This is no time for talk." With these words, he returns to sharpening his tomahawk and ignores them.

Atsan stares down at Tonda for a moment and then turns and continues walking. Tonda watches them leave, annoyed and unsettled by their conversation. As they arrive at the village gate Atsan suddenly stops and turns to his father. "I will come with you," he says, in a tone that betrays both his fear and his conviction.

Brulé stops, surprised and taken aback. Atsan explains, "Tonda is our war chief. He leads us when we fight. He carries us with his fearlessness.

Just now I saw two things. He is afraid to take this trip with you. And he does not understand what you say about guns. He cannot lead us against this enemy if he does not understand."

Brulé stares at his son, impressed by his insight. Atsan continues, "This trip is not what I want. I want to fight. But I see it is the right path. Foolish maybe, but for some reason the right path. I am coming." Brulé can hear the determination in his son's words. He looks at him, and then at Savignon. "I am proud of you, Atsan," he says, "But I cannot have you come."

"I am Wendat and your son."

Unconsciously touching the scars on his neck, Brulé shakes his head.

"What would you have me do then, make stew? Sew moccasins while you are gone?" Atsan pleads, " Take me, this time. Please."

It hurts Brulé to look at his son, so vital and healthy, and imagine what could happen on this trip. He turns to Savignon, who, holding his gaze, says what Brulé knows is true, " He is a man now, Etienne. It is time."

Brulé wraps his arm around Atsan's shoulder and pulls him tightly to his chest. It is decided.

The Marquis de Clemont splashes steaming water on his face from a bowl held steady in the hands of his obliging footman. He reaches for a towel and pats his face dry. As he finishes, he suddenly notices how filthy the towel is and throws it in disgust towards the footman. "Why is this so foul? Hurry up, pour me some wine," he orders impatiently as he walks away.

The camp hums with activity as it readies itself yet again for the night. Everything proceeds routinely and efficiently — building the palisade, erecting the tents, preparing meals.

De Clemont lazes at his table, watching the scene unfold as the footman pours him wine. He notices de Valery talking with Petashwa and calls to him, but de Valery doesn't hear, or chooses not to. De Clemont fidgets. He feels lost out here in this empty wilderness and needs someone to whom he can complain and vent his frustrations. He orders the footman to go over and fetch de Valery. The footman returns announcing that the Count is on his way. But still de Valery continues talking, as de Clemont fumes impatiently. Finally de Valery joins him.

"What can you possibly find so interesting talking with that savage?"

De Valery wants to say that at least the savage isn't constantly and incessantly complaining about his discomforts, but he holds his tongue, all too aware he'd live to regret such an outburst of honesty. He finds being with de Clemont increasingly oppressive. It is true that he does find life in the wilderness hard. Miserable, really. But after repeating it a hundred times, the statement becomes meaningless. De Valery senses that his friend feels increasingly adrift, and bereft without all the etiquette, privilege, intrigue and alliances of their former court life. De Clement clings to him as a kind of anchor. De Valery is also annoyed that everyone else is busy, engaged, and utterly ignores them. And thus he finds himself watching Petashwa, becoming more and more intrigued with the "savage". Someone he had at first dismissed as barely capable of thought or certainly intelligence, he now realizes leads the entire expedition. Officially, of course, du Barre is in command. It is du Barre who utters pronouncements and declares objectives. But it is clear to everyone, except du Barre, that Petashwa orchestrates all the day-to-day practicalities of the expedition. He confers with Champlain often but Champlain clearly has withdrawn from offering any overt leadership. The one or two times he has asserted himself, du Barre has, in front of everyone, so thoroughly crushed the initiative, he has simply retreated to his maps and drawings and journals.

Petashwa interacts smoothly with the Algonquin, the French aides, French soldiers and with du Barre. He calms disagreements between the groups and smooths negotiations. At first he had even made an effort to ensure de Valery and de Clemont were comfortable, at least until de Clemont's nasty abuse. From that point on, Petashwa has kept his distance, which only served to fuel the noble's anger. After one such temperamental outburst, de Valery had approached Petashwa to apologize on behalf of his friend. Yet despite the harsh verbal abuse, Petashwa seemed unaffected. He smiled and thanked him for his kind words. In that moment he met de Valery's eyes and held them, perhaps for a few seconds. And de Valery knew then, he trusted this man, that he certainly wasn't a savage and if he needed someone to talk to he could talk to Petashwa. He had, in fact, an ally.

Some days later, he had gone to talk with Petashwa again. Even though Petashwa spoke decent French, his words reflected an understanding of the land completely alien to de Valery. He had described the rapids that lay ahead of them and the power of the "spirit" they would feel in the rushing waters. De Valery had dismissed the idea but Petashwa was patient. He suggested, when they were there, not to think of spirit as a god, but as a power or a presence. Although skeptical de Valery had to admit, despite himself, he was anticipating the experience, actually looking forward to it.

But now, as he sat down next to de Clemont he knew he could share none of this. De Clemont pressed him about their conversation. "In two days we come to some enormous rapids and we must walk around them," was the only thing he could think to say.

"I would much prefer walking than sitting in that canoe all day. Here, play cards with me."

De Clemont deals the cards, picks up his hand and pushes his chair back so he can cross his legs. He notices a tear in his silk stocking. "Damn, another pair." Throwing his cards down, he stares out with abject hopelessness at the camp and out across the river. "What a god-forsaken place. What can we possibly tell Richelieu? 'Oh, it is charming, Your Eminence. It looks just like France. And the brutes are lining up to know God.'"

"That, I think, nicely sums up what he wants to hear."

They notice du Barre crossing the camp towards them. Both de Valery and de Clemont make the slightest effort to rise as he approaches them, then offer him a glass of wine but the priest waves it off.

Before du Barre can utter a word de Valery says, "Champlain told me that Brulé's father was the Commander de Coligny. Did you know that?"

"What? Coligny's son. The Protestant. Why didn't he tell me?"

"I remember the stories of Coligny from when I was a boy. He was the greatest field commander of his day."

61

"New France is Catholic. There will be no Protestants here," fumes du Barre.

"I suggested the same thing," de Valery continued, "but Champlain said he doubted there was much Christianity of any sort in Brulé now."

"I cannot imagine how black that soul of his must be." Then he turns on de Valery, "Just so the record is clear, the Crown sent a Catholic army, defeated Coligny and hung his body from a spike on the city wall."

De Valery senses his baiting of du Barre hits its mark and presses on. "So I heard. I was told we outnumbered him four to one, but by the end of the battle our losses were so heavy we abandoned the campaign. Hobbled home, as it were. What was left of us."

Du Barre eyes him now with rage and hisses, "What is your point?"

De Valery leans back and smiles, and offers a final prod, "I do not really have one. It was over thirty years ago. It's just that I've always admired the stories of his exploits. Someone so brave, capable…regardless of what side he was on."

Du Barre seethes, knowing he's been made to look a fool, but manages to regain his pious air. "I came over," he now states with an exaggerated affect of contentment, "hoping you would join me for Mass. It is the day of the Transformation of our Lord."

They realize they have no escape. "Yes, Father, we would be delighted," says de Clemont. And then under his breath to de Valery, but spoken just loud enough to ensure the priest can hear, "That was well done."

Brulé and Atsan have paddled hard for three days east along the north shore of Lake Ontario — the Lake of Shining Water, as the Wendat call it — to the first place they can risk crossing the wide open water to the south shore. The crossing takes a full day and both the weather and waves cooperate. On reaching the far side, they hide their canoe deep in the bushes that line the shore and continue on foot. They move quickly, silently. Brulé's learned from the Wendat warriors how to hold an awareness of everything happening around him. Not in his mind, not thinking, but a feeling of moving in a flow of change and then noticing any unusual shifts, of bird song, or smells, or pull of attention. If something breaks the pattern, he stops and waits until that sense of flow around him reasserts itself before he continues.

The Iroquois travel mainly by river to their villages. But Brulé knows that out here they could meet a hunting or scouting party anywhere and anytime. They continue until the last light fades and they can no longer see the ground clearly. The sound of a careless footfall on a large stick could be fatal. They pull themselves beneath some dense juniper bushes for shelter, eat a piece of pemmican, then close their eyes and in no time, they sleep.

A huge bonfire burns in the Iroquois village. Dozens of warriors scream and dance, shimmering in the red-orange heat of the flames. Totiri, the Iroquois war chief, approaches, a menacing smile spread across his face. He holds in front of him a red-hot axe head. Closer. Closer.

Brulé wakes with a start from the nightmare, his face covered in sweat. His abrupt move wakes Atsan. He has seen his father awakened like this before. He gently places his hand on Brulé's shoulder until he feels his breathing return to normal. Brulé regains his sense of where he is and pats Atsan's hand to let him know he has recovered. But they are awake now; the first light of morning has arrived. They crawl out from beneath the bushes. Just then a swooping whistle of wind and a large white hawk flaps once, twice and alights on a branch above them. Brulé raises his hand to the bird and smiles, "My brother, Atsan. He will look after us."

The father and son travel all that day. Sporadically, they cross Iroquois hunting trails, or sometimes clear and well-worn deer trails that look inviting to follow but lead nowhere. Once they are forced to drop low as an Iroquois hunting party, carrying two deer back to their village, passes dangerously close. Finally, by the afternoon of the third day they lay at the edge of the forest surveying the huge clearing in front of the imposing palisade of Siskwa's village. Sentries stand atop the high palisade wall.

"What do we do now?" asks Atsan.

"Not much I can do but standup and start walking. You wait here."

"No, I am coming." And with that Atsan stands up and walks into the clearing. Brulé curses and catches up. Immediately the sentries give warning. The men and women bending over their squash and bean plants in the fields stand and stare. Children whoop and yell and run towards them until a harsh call beckons them back.

The hawk circles silently above.

By the time they arrive at the village a crowd of warriors has gathered and awaits them.

"Whatever happens, do not flinch," warns Brulé as he walks directly into the mass of warriors in front of him. The Iroquois push and punch them. Some swing their clubs and axes but stop just before striking. The two men push through, taking every hit and punch, revealing no hint of either pain or fear. At last, they push through the narrow gate and find themselves free of the warriors. But immediately in the open clearing of the village they spot another group turning to face them.

Brulé holds up his hand in a gesture of peace, "We come in peace. We have come to help the Iroquois. I have come to speak with Siskwa."

Warriors approach from behind through the gate just as the warriors in front suddenly part ranks, and Totiri emerges. Half his face is painted black, the other half decorated with three vertical red stripes. The Iroquois war chief steps towards them, his threatening demeanor on full display and his menace palpable.

The presence of Totiri suddenly here, right in front of him, catches Brulé off-guard. He feels his knees give and he grabs Atsan's arm.

"So White Trader. You come back. With your boy it seems. It is my luck to travel to this village today so I can meet you again," jeers Totiri.

Brulé, recovered now, stands impassive but curses himself for revealing his fear to Totiri. Any warrior, whether Iroquois or Wendat, looks for weakness at moments like this. The war chief studies them, judging their strength and weakness. "Is it more pain you seek? Or perhaps you wish to test whether your boy is a man."

Brulé again holds up his hand in peace. "Totiri, we have come in peace to see Siskwa. Not you. This is his village."

The hawk circles lower over the men, his screeching cries pierce the air. Several warriors look up, but Totiri ignores the shrill cries. He gestures suddenly to several of his warriors who grab Brulé and Atsan, pulling them over to two stakes set in the ground. They resist, but are quickly bound, their arms tied behind the post. The warriors circle about, continually shouting and taunting them.

Totiri raises his hand for silence. "When I finish with the boy I am going to skin you alive. Like I should have the last time."

Father Marquette pushes aside the oilcloth covering the door and steps out of the chapel into the sunshine. He surveys the palisade of the Wendat village as Father LeCharon steps out of the chapel and joins him reluctantly.

"Fear not the savages, Jean-Philippe. The Lord is with us," says Marquette.

LeCharon can barely disguise his growing sense of panic. He knows they are here to convert the Wendat, but everything inside him rebels against Marquette's plan, against his certainty and fervour. "I know how frustrated we are here in our ministry but I think it wise to wait until we can talk with Brulé."

"Damn Brulé!" Marquette erupts. LeCharon has never seen him so vehement, and he tended that way by nature. "We will rot before he helps us. He has done nothing and will continue to do nothing for us. He never wanted us here and is doing everything he can to make sure we leave."

"That is true, until now, but —"

Marquette continues, "Savignon told me some of the sick could die. Particularly the young ones. We have freedom of the village. We can baptize them and if they die we bring them to our Lord at their moment of greatest need."

"But we haven't been to the village for weeks, not since those few fell sick. The way they look at us now, I —"

"We came to serve Christ," interrupts Marquette, focusing his fierce, blue eyes on LeCharon. "And that is what we will do. We vowed in coming here we would save their savage souls. For almost a year we have let Brulé and that chief continue to tell us they will help. What have we seen? Nothing. Jean-Philippe, we are the ones damned if we do not answer our Lord's call. We will be damned if we continue to do nothing. We can wait no longer. We put our trust and safety in the hands of our Lord."

With that, Marquette starts walking towards the village. LeCharon follows against his better judgement, struggling to keep up to the other priest's pace. They enter the village, each with a gourd of water. Villagers stop what they are doing and watch them cross to a longhouse and enter.

The two priests stand in the dark, smoky longhouse waiting for their eyes to adjust. A thirty-foot high arch of bent saplings, covered in bark, stretches eighty feet into the darkness. The only light enters through three smoke holes in the ceiling, down the length of the longhouse. Below each burns a small cook fire. Two tiers of storage and beds run down the wall on each side. Corn, herbs, fish, and furs hang from the ceiling just above their heads.

Two Wendat, an older woman and a girl, lay next to the fire, feverish and shivering. Open sores cover their faces and arms. Somewhere deep in the longhouse the two priests can hear the sounds of people sobbing and moaning in pain.

Bent close to the fire, Kinta, Brulé's wife, and another woman busily tend to the sick. As soon as they notice the priests, both quickly stand up and back away as if fearing reprimand. Marquette takes this as a sign of permission to help. He kneels beside the older woman and crosses himself. LeCharon hesitates but does the same, kneeling beside the girl.

Two eyes from deep inside the longhouse watch closely as Marquette lifts the woman's head, wets his finger from the gourd of water and makes a cross on her forehead as he chants in Latin.

Kinta quickly leaves the longhouse. The pair of eyes in the darkness continues to watch the priests.

After giving his first blessing, Marquette proceeds further into the longhouse towards the second cook fire. The three women attending the sick cringe from him but he remains oblivious to their reaction. He kneels now before a young boy, burning with fever and wide-eyed in terror at this strange dark figure in black robes now hovering over him.

At that moment, just as Kinta and Atironta, the Wendat chief, enter the longhouse, the eyes that have been watching emerge from the shadows. A warrior, war club in hand, is on top of Marquette in a second. The club swings down smashing the priest's head. Once. Twice. LeCharon cries out. The warrior raises his club a third time.

"Stop," Atironta's voice thunders through the longhouse.

The warrior slowly lowers his raised club and turns to Atironta, meeting his gaze, one will pitted against the other. He slides his foot under Marquette, slumped in a heap on the ground, and roughly turns him over onto his back. He kneels, grabs the crucifix from around the priest's neck, breaks the chain and throws it on the fire. Wiping his fingers in the blood oozing from Marquette's head, he draws a red cross on the priest's forehead. Then he stands, leers at LeCharon and disappears back into the shadows as quickly as he had emerged.

LeCharon watches the crucifix glow red in the fire.

The head of a steel tomahawk shimmers, as red-orange as the coals in the fire. Totiri jams a green branch into the axe head and lifts it close to his face. He smiles as he feels the searing heat near his skin. He turns and approaches Atsan, tied to the stake.

"Three times I have tortured white men. Two screamed, sobbed like children. Their fear of pain overcomes them. But I could not get your father to make a sound. Now I will decorate you the way I decorated him. And we will see how brave you are." The hawk, circling above, suddenly swoops lower.

Totiri raises the red-hot tomahawk to Atsan's neck. Atsan tenses, eyes wide. He stares at Totiri in defiance. Brulé struggles and rages against the ropes that bind him. Totiri looks at him, then back at Atsan, "If you had stayed here with me, I would have turned you into a real warrior." He leans forward, his face so close he can feel Atsan's breath, and then slowly pushes the tomahawk onto Atsan's neck. Steam and smoke hiss off his burning flesh. His body vibrates in convulsions of pain, yet he makes no sound but for the sharp exhale of breath through his clenched teeth.

Once again, the hawk cries out, descending yet lower, beating his wings just above them. The Iroquois warriors stare at the hawk and at one another. They are alarmed; they know why the hawk is there and can feel its power. But Totiri ignores it, continuing to stare into Atsan's face. Atsan glares back unyielding, his eyes wild with pain. Totiri smiles again as he turns the tomahawk over. A fresh surface of red-hot metal sears Atsan's neck. As the cloud of smoke and steam hisses off his flesh, a rock strikes Totiri's face knocking him back a step. The tomahawk drops to the ground.

"Touch him again, and I will kill you."

In front of the entrance to the nearest longhouse stands a woman. She's regal, with a weathered beauty and as wild as a cougar in her rage as she confronts Totiri. "Get away from him."

"N…Nuttah," stammers Brulé. Atsan, attempting to see through the haze of smoke and pain, perceives the outline of the woman. Even in his crazed, pain-wracked awareness, he has heard Brulé speak her name and realizes immediately who this must be. Siskwa, the Iroquois chief, comes out of the longhouse and stands now beside the woman. The hawk lands atop the stake holding Brulé, beating its wings slowly, unsure yet whether to stay or again alight.

Siskwa looks at Totiri, "You disgrace us. This is not your village to act like this. Is your hate and jealousy so great you cannot see the power of the spirit these men bring," pointing at the hawk. "You know they come in peace."

He dismisses Totiri with a gesture and then with another indicates to the warriors to cut Brulé and Atsan loose. He beckons Brulé.

Totiri bristles at his humiliation. He and Brulé glare at each other in hate-honed anger. As Nuttah quickly moves towards Brulé, the war chief eyes the woman with equal fury, takes three swift steps and smashes her across the face. Enrages, Brulé charges at Totiri, but several Iroquois manage to hold him back. Totiri casts one last menacing look at them and walks away.

Brulé approaches Nuttah, gripped by a turmoil of emotion. He touches her face where she has been struck. Nuttah takes his hand, "Go. Talk with Siskwa. I will care for Atsan." She pushes him gently in the direction of the longhouse. The hawk now beats its powerful wings several times as it rises from the post where Brulé had been tied, swoops down in one last dive above Brulé's head and then, climbing fast, disappears beyond the village wall.

Inside the longhouse, the chief gestures for Brulé to join him beside the fire. He lights a pipe, smokes briefly and hands it to Brulé. "Totiri is best in battle. He seems to create trouble everywhere else. I am sorry." He takes the pipe Brulé has offered back to him and sits smoking for a moment and then continues, "Nuttah, that Wendat woman, Totiri's wife. She was your wife."

Brulé nods, another rush of rage as he learns they are married.

"But you have not come because of her?"

He shakes his head.

"And that boy. He is your son. Her son."

Again Brulé nods, unable to talk, consumed by mounting waves of conflicting emotion. Siskwa, perceiving Brulé's turmoil, continues to smoke his pipe, looking into the fire. "Deep currents of spirit unfold here today." Then he asks, "So tell me, White Trader, why have you come?"

With the gentle care of a mother, Nuttah softly pats grease onto the red-blistered flesh on Atsan's neck with the tips of her fingers. With her other hand she clutches his arm. Both look into the other's eyes, beseeching, beyond their discomfort, beyond their awkwardness, as if despite the strangeness, they might retrieve all the lost years of the other's being.

Eventually the weight of his questions outweigh the mesmerizing grip of his mother's presence, and Atsan stammers, "I was told you were dead. Why did you not come home? Escape. What are you doing here?" As a Wendat warrior he would never allow himself to be caught crying but now, despite himself, tears roll down his cheeks.

"I tried, years ago. It is not so easy as that."

"But why didn't he come and get you?"

"You know the story. He must have told you."

"He told me you were dead."

"He was almost dead by the time Totiri had finished with him. He did not know if I lived."

"But you must come with us now. I cannot leave here without you."

"I have two children, Atsan."

"With that demon!"

"Girls. They need me more than you do. You are a man now. A Wendat. A man any mother would be proud of."

Atsan listens, anguished at the reality he must somehow digest.

"What about my sister? What happened to her?"

"She married a good man and has a small boy. Her place is here now."

"An Iroquois...a good man! How can you say that?"

"They are not so different than us, Atsan. At least most of them."

"Your sister lives in this village. That is why I came here to visit," explains Nuttah. "That at least is what I told Totiri. I see what these guns do to him and what he plans against the Wendat. All I could think to do is talk to Siskwa. Your father also it seems."

"You have the courage of a great chief," Siskwa says to Brulé, "I can see that. In spite of what the Iroquois did to you the last time, yet for your people, the Wendat, you risk this. I fear you are right about a war with guns between us. It will bring more violence with the Wendat as certain as the rushing rivers of spring. Would your Wendat chiefs agree to this? I think not. We are all too proud. And too bound by fear and mistrust.

"The English traders came here. To trade guns," continues Siskwa. "They spoke, as you say, of destroying our enemies."

"You trust the English?" asks Brulé.

"They speak of destroying enemies in the same way we see them destroy the land. No, it is not about trust." Siskwa stops a moment, considering, then continues, "I will tell you. We have few furs left for trade, many of our people are sick, and die with a disease our shamans cannot heal. We have new enemies to the south and the west. The white man, the English, push into our hunting grounds to the east."

"Then why do they sell you guns?"

He motions to a warrior, sitting nearby in the shadows, to bring him a musket. Placing it on his lap, he strokes its dark, oiled wood and gleaming black metal. "When I first held the white man's metal knife, I felt its edge.

I felt its power. I wanted it like nothing I had ever seen before. Our own stone knives seemed foolish. And then we wanted the white man's axes. And his kettles. The women had to have them too. And the needles, the coloured cloth, and the beads and the blankets. The white man's hold on us is invisible but the grip is like that of the jaws of a wolf." He lifts the gun. "And now the muskets. I see it in the eyes of the young men. They lust after them as they lust after a beautiful woman. They want them. No chief can control that. The English have seen that lust. They gamble that we will destroy our enemies and not our source for more guns. The white man casts a long shadow on the Iroquois way of life. And on the Wendat way of life."

The old chief lowers his head again and looks into the fire. "I am sorry, White Trader. I have heard of you often. I wish we could talk when the waters around us were not so rough, so dangerous."

As Brulé emerges out of Siskwa's longhouse, he sees Atsan and Nuttah huddled together by the gate to the village and walks towards them, aware that for Atsan, the world has changed. He has stood at an Iroquois torture stake, the most terrifying assault imaginable and then experienced the deep comfort of a lost mother, only now to be separated from her again.

The emotions in his own chest churn. As he reaches them, Nuttah turns and, like two magnets, they rush to embrace — ten years of lost love desperate to be recovered. Catching herself, Nuttah abruptly pulls away, wiping tears from her eyes. "I will pay a heavy price for this," as she looks into Brulé's eyes, sharing a deep, wordless communication they had once enjoyed. Then with all the strength in her being, she turns and leaves. As she walks back into the village, she does not dare look behind her.

Atsan grabs his father's arm, but Brulé leans in close to his son and warns, "Not now. We must get away. We are still not safe."

The two exit through the gate. The warriors, still lingering near the entrance, eye them suspiciously but give them a wide berth to pass freely. Brulé and his son purposely make a point not to rush, even as their backs prickle with a sense of imminent danger behind them. As they approach near to the edge of the forest they quicken their pace. The moment they are safe in the shelter of the trees, Atsan explodes in a fury of confusion and pain, finally able to release his terror and anguish. He kneels and pounds the ground with his fist. "She is my mother, my mother! Living here with the Iroquois. How could you let her? Why didn't you tell me?" cries Atsan.

"I thought she was dead. I didn't know. When Totiri finished with me, I lost consciousness. I only came to lying on the ground outside the village. Alone. I never saw her. I —"

"She told that beast she would marry him."

Brulé feels like a knife is driven into his heart when he hears these words. He knows this means only one thing: Nuttah had sacrificed herself to keep him alive. All the events that had led to that moment when his broken body screamed back into awareness as he lay in the mud outside the village, now return to haunt him. The door he had so firmly shut now opens like a floodgate. He cannot stop his wild howl of anguish.

"I never thought we would see her again. Not here. Not today…not ever."

Atsan shares with him his mother's warning, "She told me, they have forty guns and plan to attack the Wendat. Soon."

"Atsan, we had to know that number. But the price you had to pay for us to get it. You were defiant. You were fearless. Any Wendat warrior would be proud of how you stood up to him. You must be wracked by all this today, but we will get guns, Atsan, and we will crush Totiri."

It's dusk in the camp. With the palisade built and all in order, members of the expedition relax, eating their evening meal in the gathering dark. While others squat on the ground, Champlain sits with the nobles at their elaborately set table. The footman returns with a silver tray. On it rest three porcelain bowls, each with a dollop of gruel. De Clemont eyes the dinner. "Now less than three weeks into this nightmare all our provisions are gone. We came from France well stocked. But no, you must cut back. It would be too heavy for these brutes to carry." He pokes at the thick mush and puts his spoon down. "Look at this slop."

"Come Monsieur Le Marquis, it will toughen you up," jokes Champlain.

"I am not interested in being toughened up. I am interested in going home. You know what I am going to do when I get home? Do you remember, Jean-Marie, that dish the Duchess de Nantes served that time? That small hen stuffed with fish and mushrooms. When I get home I am going to invite myself over and tell her how I dreamed of that dish out in this god-forsaken waste."

"Ah yes, that does sound good," says Champlain. "Unfortunately, we do not have the leisure to hunt for game now to supplement our diet. We must make time." He looks at the dancing refractions of the candles through the delicate glass of the decanter. "And thank you for inviting me to join you for the last of the wine. That was very kind," says Champlain.

"But you were saying about Savignon. Please continue," de Valery encourages him.

"I was just saying, can you imagine for Savignon, coming from this wilderness, not yet twenty, going to the French court. Everything must have been so overwhelming, like a dream. Anne-Marie was fifteen then, playful, charming. She helped steer him through it."

"He does have good taste," says de Clemont.

"I was only five at the time but I remember meeting him. The savage from the New World, they called him. My parents took me to see him. But he did not strike me as savage, especially dressed in court attire."

"The Jesuits got hold of him for awhile," continued Champlain, "hoping to convert him so he might help them back here. But he hated being with the priests and even managed to return to court for awhile before the Jesuits shipped him back to Québec. They hoped and believed that once he saw the way his people lived, after his exposure to civilization and Christianity, that he would be inspired to help convert them. But to their great chagrin, he escaped within a couple of weeks with the next trading party and returned to the Wendat.

"He often joins the trading group to Québec hoping I think that he might be able to go back to France. Or that Anne-Marie might have come to see him. She still sends him a coat every year. I have it with me to give him."

Champlain sips his wine, and then, aware he has the nobles' attention, continues, "When Savignon first came back he asked me if I thought he could buy Anne-Marie."

The nobles sit up in alarm.

"Buy! Whatever do you mean?"

"For thirty beaver pelts. It was a lot at the time. At least for him."

The nobles are aghast, horrified. "Buy the Duchess Anne-Marie de Navarre? With furs?" The idea is absurd to their European ears, an affront to their entire world-view. To their mind, this wasn't a dowry among peers so much as a brutal kind of animal barter.

"He was caught between two worlds. Imagine Savignon trying to describe the French court to the Wendat using the words he would have from a life here — a palace hall covered in gilded murals, the scale of it. Or a horse-drawn carriage when they have never seen a horse, a wheel or roads. When he started telling them these stories, they simply laughed at him. Brulé was the only one who could understand what he had been through."

"Well, personally I would say he was mad — thinking you could buy a duchess with a few beaver skins."

"It is ironic," continues Champlain, "how the lives of Savignon and Brulé mirror each other. A Wendat who longs to be in France and a Frenchman who longs to be in this wilderness. At least Brulé is here, where he wants to be."

"But why is he out here? Why would anyone choose this?" asks de Clemont. "It seems absurd."

"The first year we were here, it was 1609. We had no idea what winter would be like. No one could have imagined the cold. Brulé had spent much of the summer with the Algonquin, hunting and learning their language. Their language is devilishly difficult to understand. I have spent twenty-five years trying to learn it and still I can express only the most basic ideas. But Brulé just seemed to understand it. That first winter he hunted and helped keep us in food. Even so, only eleven of us survived. Of thirty-eight. A Wendat trading party arrived to exchange goods with the Algonquin the next summer and Brulé took one look at them, I think, and saw his future.

"The Wendat brought excellent furs. I knew the fur trade might help support us here, I still hoped then we might find a route to the Indies, and I needed someone who could translate for me. So I sent him off.

"The Wendat were worried that if anything happened to him, we would be angry. I assured them that would not be the case but I do not think they quite trusted me. So they sent one of the chief's sons to stay with us. That was Savignon and we immediately sent him to France on the next ship.

"I remember that the following summer Brulé was supposed to arrive back with the trading party. But I looked in each canoe as it came to shore and failed to see him; I was seriously worried something had happened. But then suddenly, there he was standing right in front of me, looking so much like a Wendat I could not tell them apart.

"I remember taking him aside and scolding him that we were in New France to civilize the savages, not become like them. But it was obviously too late. He spoke Wendat well and the people loved him. He traded very fairly for them too. He refused to let them waste their furs in exchange for useless trinkets. I was furious at the time but over the years we and the

81

Wendat have grown to trust each other because of it.

"He slid into their way of life completely. Each year he would return with the trading party, full of stories. He could hold a room spellbound with his adventures. He even married a Wendat woman, had children…"

"Married a savage?"

"She was the most sought after woman in all the Wendat villages, Savignon told me. Brulé won her heart."

De Clemont catches de Valery's eye and smirks. "Ah, a savage dish I'm sure."

"That was his first wife."

Both de Clemont and de Valery wait expectantly.

"About ten years ago Brulé stopped coming to Québec. I worried he had been hurt or even killed, but the Wendat assured me he was fine. When he finally did return to Québec, he was changed. Darker. Withdrawn. He would tell me nothing, but he had terrible scars, burns, all over his neck and chest. Eventually Savignon told me what had happened.

"While Brulé was far away to the west on a trading expedition, an Iroquois raiding party attacked a Wendat fishing camp. Nuttah, Brulé's wife, and his two children were taken. When he returned he gathered what clues he could and somehow pieced together the trail back to the village of the Iroquois who had taken them. I think a number of Wendat joined him. But they could not attack the village and so they waited, watching for days.

"The Wendat lost patience and returned home. Only Savignon stayed with Brulé. He said they lay there for weeks in hiding and then one day he saw Atsan, his son, playing in the fields with some of the boys of the village. He would have been seven or eight by then, I think. Brulé managed to grab him and escape and brought him home. But he wanted his wife, and decided to go back. All the Wendat warned him not to go. But he went. Savignon was the only one to join him and again, for weeks they were in hiding, watching the village.

"Eventually, despite everything Savignon tried to do to stop him, Brulé hatched a plan to sneak inside the village. After awhile, Savignon knew something had gone wrong but did not know what to do. He said he wept when he saw what crawled away from the village that night."

"After that, for God's sake, why would he not go back to France? Get away from all this," asked de Valery.

"He changed. That is sure. But I think he somehow connected even more deeply to the life here; I cannot explain it. But he spent more and more time going further and further into the wilderness. The excuse he gave of course was that it was for the fur trade. And it was good for trade — new sources of fur from new and more distant tribes. Yet I think he found something out there, something he tried to explain to me one time. He talked of spirit, of the Great Spirit, but certainly not any spirit that a Christian would know. He actually told me he had found Paradise."

"Paradise?" said de Clemont. "I thought Paradise was lost, not found."

"It is the English who have given this idea to the Iroquois," explains Brulé, who, immediately upon his return, has gone straight to talk with Atironta. "Not only to fight, but to conquer. Take our land. They want our fur routes. The English get the furs, but let the Iroquois soil their hands with our blood." This was the inevitable conclusion Brulé had come to after reflecting on what Siskwa had told him. He felt the chief had wanted him to know. Maybe he didn't want to see that fierce, honorable rivalry between the Iroquois and the Wendat, one he had lived with, and his father, and his father before him, destroyed in a flurry of shameful English bullets.

"But if we are inside the village, what can guns do to us?" asks Atironta.

"They burn our crops, village by village," answers Brulé. "This is the white man's warfare. Destruction. The Iroquois will learn it quickly enough."

Just then Savignon enters the longhouse. "Father LeCharon said he wanted to see you as soon as you returned. He wants to talk to Atironta."

"Tell him we can talk later," replies Brulé.

"He is outside now. He is desperate, Etienne."

Brulé glances at Atironta, who looks up at Savignon and nods. The clubbing of the priest has weighed heavily on the chief's mind and heart; he has anticipated this conversation with apprehension. Savignon leads the priest into the longhouse. LeCharon looks haggard, lean, his eyes bloodshot. Atironta motions for him to sit with them by the fire. LeCharon watches and fidgets restlessly as Atironta lights his pipe. After several puffs, the chief passes it on to LeCharon but the priest cannot restrain his impatience. "I want this man punished," he bursts out. "There must be justice."

Atironta looks up. Brulé motions for the priest to calm down. He knows that such an emotional outburst, acceptable in the culture of the white man, will be perceived as a terrible breach of custom to the Wendat, who when faced with internal conflict, sit together quietly, smoke the pipe, and build, however slowly, a sense of common purpose towards a common resolution.

Brulé tries his best to intervene. After translating for Atironta, he tells LeCharon, "Justice is a difficult word to translate in Wendat — at least in the way that you mean it."

"Of course they have no word for justice because they are damned and heathen wretches living in chaos."

"No, I mean your idea of justice and the punishment you want."

"Yes, punished, exactly!" exclaims LeCharon. The priest, he knows, understands but one view of justice and that view is bound to another for punishment — and a very specific, brutal kind of punishment.

"Try to understand how the Wendat approach this. We have a grave imbalance —"

"Balance! You cannot protect this barbarian with such mindless drivel. He is a criminal. He clubbed Father Marquette when he was saving that boy from damnation."

"Marquette was about to baptize his son, taking him to the French Land of the Dead. In the father's mind that is the worst nightmare he could imagine," clarifies Brulé.

"Superstitious rot!" LeCharon spits in anger. "We offered the Wendat Heaven and in exchange you give us chaos and misery."

"I have heard of this heaven from Savignon. Your Land of the Dead," says Atironta.

Brulé translates the chief's comment for LeCharon. The priest corrects him, "Heaven is not a Land of the Dead. We live there in glory with our Lord, Jesus Christ, in His Kingdom."

"That little dead man on the stick?" asks Atironta, incredulous. LeCharon shakes his head in disgust; he is dealing with a child.

"No, Heaven is there," he points to the sky.

Atironta looks up, perplexed. "How far?" the chief asks. "How do you get there?"

Hearing Brulé's translation, LeCharon is stunned; he cannot believe the question. "Is he really that stupid?"

Brulé closes his eyes and takes a deep breath, desperately trying not to react to the priest's rigid, pious arrogance. "You do nothing to understand the Wendat."

"In the Lord's name what do you want me to understand about this savage witchcraft of theirs?"

"You could start by trying to understand the Wendat Land of the Dead."

LeCharon heaves with frustration and rage at this useless exchange, at Father Marquette's condition and his own fear of being left alone, abandoned, in this grim hellhole.

"Fine. Where is the Wendat Land of the Dead?" he asks Brulé who translates for Atironta.

"There," Atironta points west, "where the sun hides herself in the evening."

"How far?" asks the priest.

"Three days," answers Atironta.

"How do you get there?"

"On foot."

LeCharon glares at Brulé and rolls his eyes. Turning to Atironta he states what, for him, is an irrefutable truth, "You will burn in the flames of Hell forever in your Land of the Dead."

The chief listens as Brulé translates and then levels an intense, penetrating gaze directly at LeCharon. "No Wendat is coward enough to fear the torture of your Christian hell."

Brulé laughs at the audacity of the chief's words. The statement stops LeCharon in his tracks. His fear of hell is absolute. His mouth hangs open, speechless. Atironta continues, "You feel the Wendat attacked your friend for no reason. But our Land of the Dead is real to us just as yours is real to you. That warrior believed he would never see his son again. That his son would live with your black robes forever. You —"

"He must be punished. He must go to prison or be hanged," interrupts LeCharon, increasingly unnerved by the direction of this exchange.

For a second time now, Atironta is taken aback by the priest's high-minded rudeness; interrupting another person as they speak is the height of disrespect to the Wendat way. Even more so, interrupting a chief. Atironta is losing patience with the priest and his narrow, dogmatic solutions, and a world-view so rigidly opposed to his own. Brulé looks at Atironta, who nods for him to continue translating. Brulé stops at the word 'prison', searching for a way to explain it.

He tells Atironta, "The man must be put in a cage." Then he turns to the priest, "Do you see any prisons here, Charon?"

"Not here. But I visited that other village with Savignon and there was a man in a cage. A small cage."

"Iroquois," says Brulé.

"What difference does that make?"

"A Wendat would never do that to a Wendat."

"I want that savage in a cage."

Brulé shakes his head. "And I have no word in Wendat for 'hang', to hang someone the way you mean."

"How can you live in this lawless nightmare?" He points a finger at Brulé, "but I will make them pay for this."

Brulé realizes how hopeless it is to imagine the priest will even try to understand the Wendat concept of justice. For even in the most serious circumstance, the elders, Atironta, the man accused, LeCharon, and Marquette if he was able, would sit and talk. They would talk it through until a solution was discovered to restore balance to which everyone, including LeCharon, and Marquette, could agree. Brulé had no idea precisely what that solution would be — perhaps, for the Wendat warrior, exile to another village, a terrible disgrace. But if, in the end, they all agreed, balance could be restored, and justice achieved.

Brulé could see that LeCharon would not budge. He was locked into his own idea of justice — jail or punishment by hanging — and would never find peace of mind with anything less.

"Your friend was our guest," says Atironta. "We have failed badly. For that I am sorry. But I tell you, we think you are sorcerers. We fear you. Some of our people are sick. We wonder, is it you who bring this sickness we cannot heal?"

LeCharon blurts out, "But we are not —" The chief holds up a hand for silence so firmly and with such a regal grip on the energy between them that the priest falls silent. Atironta continues in Wendat, "You wish for," he looks to Brulé for the word, "justice? You think we will have balance if we put this Wendat in a cage so he feels the misery you feel. I see your idea, the more misery he feels, the more justice you feel. This restores nothing. As chief, I must find a way to restore balance. I do not yet know how. Maybe this Wendat could take your oaths and become Christian. You want that. He would be your first. But I am not sure. We must give it more thought and act wisely."

As Brulé translates for LeCharon, the priest cannot contain himself. He blurts out, "This is wrong. That man must be punished. There must be justice." He's seething, as much out of his own fear and uncertainty as for the crime against Marquette. He turns now on Brulé. "You were supposed to help us," he hisses. "You said you would show us how to work with them. This is your fault, you know that. You are the cause of this."

"Charon, you do not listen. You never listen. When you arrived I did everything to help. They welcomed you when you came. They offered you their longhouses to live in, and their women to help you learn Wendat. But you rejected their offers. You wanted to live apart. You insulted them. And I told you how they reacted. But you did not listen. You saw only one way, your way. They had to change to suit you. But I tell you they think you and your kind are no smarter than dogs because of your beards. I told you that but did you shave? No! And your robes. They see only evil sorcerers. And the cross. And that damn bell!" He raises his hands in exasperation and then nods to Savignon.

Savignon grips LeCharon gently by the arm, and lifts him to his feet. The priest realizes he is being dismissed, the meeting is over, the meeting where he had planned to get justice for Father Marquette and have that black-hearted savage hang for his actions. And now he is being led out with nothing. Nothing. "You will burn in hell. Do you hear me? Forever." He lashes out with these last words at Brulé as Savignon maneuvers him from the longhouse.

"Champlain will be furious about this. The black robes will want revenge. And it will be me they will blame," Brulé tells Atironta.

"The black robes say no guns unless the Wendat take their spirit-man, this Christ."

"Québec needs the fur trade. They need us. Champlain would never let Québec fall because of the Jesuits. All because of one of their religious rules. But attacking the priest…" He trails off, distracted by another idea that he has wrestled with since leaving Siskwa's village. "Tell me Atironta, do I bring doom to the Wendat? If I get guns or if I do not, both condemn me."

Atironta sits quietly for a long time. He watches the glowing embers in the fire and smokes his pipe, then turns to Brulé. "White Hawk, you are a brother to our people. For that we love you. You have made it possible to trade with the white man so they do not ruin us the way they have ruined the Algonquin. For that we love you. But I will tell you now something I have never told you before.

"When you first came to us so many summers ago, I had a dream. In it the Iroquois came upon us breathing fire, scorching our people, our villages, our land until all was smoke and ash. I could not understand this dream. And I told no one. But now I see its meaning, and why I had that dream when you came to us. Because it is the white man behind that fire and ash. It is the white man that is our ruin. Not the Iroquois."

Brulé sits slouched, absorbing the wise chief's words, feeling the burden that rests on his shoulders for the vision laid out before him. There is really no way to respond to Atironta. He sees now he is called to the destruction of the Iroquois, and the Wendat. Tears well up in his eyes.

"I do bring flame and ash to the Wendat…whether we win or lose."

"No brother," continues Atironta, seeing Brulé's grief, "that dream speaks the truth. But it does not lay blame."

"Yet I forge it myself."

"Fate sometimes gives us a destiny we do not ask for. But we sing the songs of the warriors for their courage in following the destiny handed them. Your acts would be songs for the sacred fire of our people. Those songs create the bond that protects our people and feed young warriors the purpose that keeps them sharp. This is your destiny, White Hawk. If not you, who?"

Brulé has known since leaving Siskwa's village that he must get guns. Still, the idea torments him. But he knows Atironta has spoken the truth. It is too late to worry about blame, and honour, and vows from the past, and right and wrong. Fate has laid this mantle on him.

Atironta immediately addresses a practical issue. "I have seen what we trade for axes and blankets. These muskets will need many more furs than we have."

Brulé has the all important answer to that problem, "I have gold, Atironta. The white man loves gold. It is better than furs."

"You have enough to buy these guns?"

"I trade with the French for you. The French pay me in gold. Year after year. That is their way. I have enough gold to protect the Wendat."

Atironta nods, knowing this is something between white men he doesn't really understand. Brulé had shown him the gold coins before, but he could think of no practical use for it. He sits quietly for some time. Then he says, "You should take Tonda."

"There is no one else I would rather have with me if we meet Iroquois. But if Tonda knows they are coming here, he will want to stay to protect the villages."

"True, but your journey cannot fail. We cannot waste the extra weeks traveling by the north route. So you could meet Iroquois as they travel here. Tonda should join you."

Atironta rises and walks with Brulé to the doorway of the longhouse. Both Atsan and Savignon stand to greet them as they approach.

"So we go," says Brulé. "Tomorrow. Just the three of us and Tonda."

"Tonda!" exclaims Atsan, clearly happy to have him along.

"He will not be happy that I am joining you," says Savignon.

"My friend, he will learn how courageous you are. And true. I would never leave without you. With just the four of us we will travel light and fast and hope the Iroquois will be over-confident and reckless with their new guns, and we will slip around them."

In his longhouse later that afternoon, Brulé removes the woven baskets under his sleeping ledge and digs into the hard-packed earth with his tomahawk. With a few strokes he hits metal. Clearing away more dirt, he retrieves a small metal box. Inside, are two heavy leather bags. He unties one and pours a stream of gold coins into his palm.

Just then a bell rings. Brulé swings around, cursing. Quickly replacing the box under the bed, he bolts for the door.

LeCharon hangs his head, eyes closed, as he yanks the rope on the bell beside the chapel door. The loud, piercing peel reverberates in the clearing. He is so self-absorbed, he fails to notice the Wendat men approaching across the field from the village until they are but a few feet away. He looks up just as one of the men shoves LeCharon so hard he stumbles forward, hitting the chapel wall. The bell clangs erratically. A second Wendat pushes him again and he falls to the ground.

Cowering, he raises his hands as if pleading, shocked and confused by the sudden appearance of the Wendat as they stand threateningly above him. Tonda grabs LeCharon's robe and hauls him to his feet. He raises his fist to strike the priest, but just as he is about to swing, Brulé catches his arm. Tonda, thwarted, turns his rage now towards Brulé. But Brulé pulls in so close to the war chief he can't strike.

"Let me deal with that dogface," whispers Brulé. "You will bring ruin and disgrace to the Wendat if you do this."

Slowly the fire seeps out of Tonda's eyes, the tension in his body releasing. He turns a ferocious glare at LeCharon, lets go of his robe, pulls his arm free of Brulé's grip and turns to walk away. The bell rings its last fitful notes as the other Wendat follow behind Tonda back to the village.

LeCharon is about to speak when Brulé slaps him hard across the face. "You are such a god-damn fool," he says. "I have told you how they react to that bell. You have seen it before. What are you trying to do?"

"I rang it for Father Marquette. When I came back he was dead."

Brulé lets out a long sigh and slumps down onto a nearby log. He drops his head to his hands.

"He…" LeCharon's lower lip quivers and tears fill his eyes.

Brulé looks up at him, "I'm sorry."

The priest muffles a cry, "Father Marquette lived for our Lord, and these savages' salvation. We could have saved them. But you turned them against us. You…", but here his rage runs out, turns to grief and he is reduced to sobs.

Brulé feels a deep sadness seep into his being. He's exhausted by everything about these priests and their zealous need to change the Wendat. He watches LeCharon, now without Marquette's rigid stability to bolster him, casting about alone, afraid and confused.

He suddenly stands, "I leave for Québec tomorrow morning. You will have to come with me. I cannot leave you here. They will kill you before I get back. Bury Marquette. Take what you need, then I will burn this place. The Wendat hate it. You will not come back."

Early the next morning with sunlight just touching the hilltops across the river, Brulé stands with Kinta outside the village. They watch as two-dozen sick, either walking on their own or carried, are slowly being led to huts deep in the woods. They are being relocated as the shaman Okatwan had advised. Kinta lays her head on Brulé's chest and he puts his arms around her. "We could never have children, Etienne. But I can be mother to my people and care for them when they are sick."

He holds her. "I am proud to call you my wife, Kinta."

Kinta pushes away from him to look into his face. "You must come back. If you were gone…." She can't finish.

They embrace once more before Kinta leaves his side to join the sick as they head for the forest. Brulé watches her slender figure, ever straight and determined, move into the distance. She turns to wave one last time before disappearing into the trees.

Brulé then makes his way down to the shore of the river where Atsan, Savignon, Tonda, LeCharon and two canoes await him. The crucifix that had hung above the door of the chapel floats out on the lake.

"I am bringing that crucifix," wails LeCharon to Brulé. "Tonda hurled it into the lake."

Tonda looks from the priest to Brulé, "Evil spirits. Both of them."

"If you bring it, Charon, you carry it."

Part 2

On the far side of the lake, the setting sun casts the tops of the trees in a soft gold while just below, everything else now lies in shadow. A slight breeze murmurs through the trees, filling the evening air with the dense fragrance of pine and cedar. It ripples the water; arabesques of light dance over its dark surface. Atsan ladles stew from a kettle into a wooden bowl and hands it to his father. Savignon opens a tin box and takes out a china bowl and blackened silver spoon. He hands the bowl to Atsan.

"Your time with the Jesuits refined you, Savignon," Father LeCharon observes.

"What, this?" says Savignon, taking the bowl back from Atsan. "A dainty bowl for a savage, is that what you mean?"

"Well, no, I meant the experience civilized you."

"The whole experience was a curse."

"A knowledge and love of the Lord. A curse?"

"My love was for a duchess, Father. Not the Lord."

"So you too were blinded by the glitter of court." LeCharon pauses, reflecting a moment, then adds, "Like so many."

Atsan hands the priest a bowl of stew. He takes a spoonful, "Ah, meat."

"Porcupine. Enjoy it. This will be the last time we risk lighting a fire." LeCharon digs in, famished. He sucks meat from a bone and throws it in the fire. Tonda yells at him. Savignon pulls the bone out of the fire with a stick, explaining, "We keep the bones, bury them together. Then Porcupine knows we honor him and he offers himself to us again."

LeCharon snorts. "Superstitious nonsense! After all your instruction, did you come away with nothing?"

"Not really. At court I learned to eat with a knife and fork, and I learned to like French clothes. Neither much use here."

"No, I mean your religious training with the Jesuit. Did you learn nothing?"

"They scared me with their stories of hell and damnation. It still haunts me."

"As it does me. That at least is the kernel of truth."

"No, Father, that is the saddest thing of all."

"But why? It shows you the need for salvation, for God. Where do you find God otherwise? To whom do you pray, and worship?"

Savignon makes a broad gesture above him.

"Yes, exactly, you need God."

"No, I mean the sky."

"What do you mean, that the sky is your god?"

Savignon realizes that would be inaccurate, at least in terms the priest might understand. "No, not exactly. Aataentsic lives there."

"So he is your god."

"She."

"She!" Savignon enjoys watching the priest's incredulity. "And she is the one who you worship, and she protects you."

"No, generally she wants to harm us."

"What? But who protects you? You must believe someone protects you."

"Her son, Iouskeha. He created the rivers and lakes, and makes sure the crops grow."

"Ah, so he is like your creator... who gives you life."

"That would be oki."

"Oki? Who is that?"

"That isn't a who. Oki is the spirit that lives in everything. A great warrior has great oki. The rivers have oki. The rocks. The animals. Everything has oki. The porcupine has oki and so we honor him." Savignon knows he is confusing the priest and enjoys it. What he says is true, but he knows he doesn't clarify much.

LeCharon feels Savignon must be muddled about all this and asks, "Who instructs you? Who are your priests?"

Atsan, who's been listening all the while, now responds, "Instructs us? About what?"

"About God. How do you become worthy to know Him?"

"Worthy?"

"Yes, we are not worthy. That is why He sent us His Son, Our Lord Jesus Christ, because through Him we can know God."

"He is your dead man on the torture stake."

"But He is not dead. He is resurrected. He..."

He trails off, realizing he is loosing the thread of what he had wanted to say. "We need to understand our place in the world. God gives us command, mastery, over nature, including the animals. He gives us the porcupine for food. You don't need to honor a dead porcupine."

"You mean," asks Atsan, "your god makes you ruler, like a king, of nature?"

"Yes, in a way." replies the priest.

Atsan laughs at the idea and Tonda who hasn't understood anything, asks Atsan why he is laughing. When Atsan tries to explain, Tonda doesn't understand the idea of a king, an idea of leadership quite different to a chief, and when Atsan describes it, he responds, "If we leave him out here alone we would see how long he would last as king of nature."

In all the time the priests had been living with the Wendat they had never asked Savignon about his religion like this. Because he was the only one, other than Brulé and Atsan, who spoke French, they had sought him out to talk to. But all their efforts, or at least Marquette's, who dictated the conversations, had been directed towards converting him. This was, he realized, the longest conversation about his beliefs he'd had with either of them in a year.

Seeing both Atsan and Tonda laugh at him, the priest again picks up another bone from his stew, sucks it clean and then deliberately throws it in the fire. Tonda gives him a vicious blow sending him sprawling backward. Atsan gets up, once again picks the bone from the fire and sits down.

LeCharon looks up at Savignon, then Brulé, looking for some kind of sympathy, help or justice. Blood trickles from his mouth. Brulé feels sorry for LeCharon, for his confusion and the pain so evident in his face. But what made him even sadder were the porcupine bones. Even though the Wendat still practiced collecting and burying the bones of their kill, Brulé had watched as that fine sacred interplay between hunter and hunted had begun to unravel. This was hardly evident yet to the Wendat themselves. But as the fur trade had grown, he had watched as animals were stripped from the forest for goods, for the white man's goods. And now, on this trip to Québec in particular, he felt keenly aware of his role in the slow erosion of their ancient way of life.

LeCharon, unsure what to do, but desperate to get away from the anger directed at him, scrambles to his feet and heads into the woods. With every step, dead branches snap underfoot.

"The king makes more noise than a moose," says Tonda, and the others laugh.

The priest keeps walking, moving further and further into the dark forest. He can still see the fire flickering through the trees and hear the murmur of voices. He knows he needs to pray. He feels lost, adrift, spiritually empty, wracked by the death of Father Marquette. His sorrow wells up; he tries to hold back his tears, afraid that such weakness will be discovered by the others. But now for the first time his grief at losing his friend unleashes and he sobs uncontrollably. How can he return to Québec without him, their ministry a catastrophe? What price will he pay for that? With the church? And before God? He tries to collect himself. Through the dense foliage he notices the last trace of evening in the deep lavender of the evening sky. He kneels, then just as he bows his head to pray, he sees a flicker of movement in the dark. Not ten feet away stands a figure. How could this be? A white girl, young, innocent, in a communion dress stands, watching him.

LeCharon gasps. She turns to go. "No, wait," he pleads. He stands but in his haste he trips on his long robe. When he looks up again she is gone.

"Hello, hello. Are you there?"

He takes several steps yet deeper into the forest in pursuit of her. Then he hears a long, deep sigh. He's sure of it. He listens, frozen in his steps. He looks up again, the last trace of light now drained from the sky. Black surrounds him. And he feels it — nightfall. Its latches snap tight around him, sealed until morning. Suddenly, he feels nakedly alone and a spasm of fear clutches his heart. He hears laughter from the camp and sees the firelight flickering through the trees. Confused and afraid, he quickly retraces his steps back to camp. Going too quickly in the dark, he catches his robe on the low branches, trips on roots and rocks underfoot. He just wants to get back to the others and away from whatever lurks behind him. He stumbles into the clearing of the camp. The others still gathered around the fire, ignore him. But he notices Brulé sitting alone on an outcrop of rock overlooking the lake. LeCharon needs someone, anyone, even this man he hates. He hurries over towards him and without asking sits down next to Brulé, who glances over at him, then looks more closely. "You look like you have seen a ghost."

Despite himself, LeCharon stammers, "I ... I saw a girl.... a white girl. Just now…in the woods."

"You saw Tawiscaron. He is clever that one. He shows you what you fear most."

"I heard someone…breathing." He feels self-conscious, foolish uttering these words, but can't help himself. His fear and confusion have finally broken through his veneer of piety; he feels naked and vulnerable. For the first time Brulé sees the man, not the priest, now desperate for some kind of answer, some explanation as to what has clearly shaken him to his core.

"You must listen, Charon, to what is around you. Behind the songs of the birds and the wind, behind the sound of your own thoughts, you can hear her — a living, breathing spirit."

Terrified with the direction the conversation is going, feeling his vulnerability, LeCharon marshals and thrusts forward with his Christian certainty, "Spirit lies only in our Lord, Brulé."

"You have lived close to her for a year. Perhaps more has seeped in than you realize."

A rising panic grips LeCharon at the thought of his Christian anchor loosening its hold still further. Mentally he lunges desperately for something unassailable, a familiar thread he can grasp on to. "This spirit of which you speak is the devil and will lead you right to hell." He feels better, reassured for having found something forceful to speak out in his confusion.

"No, Charon. Spirit breaths here. And she speaks…if you listen."

LeCharon shivers , "What a savage, God-forsaken land."

Okatwan, the shaman, stares at the coals of his fire. Thunder rolls overhead. He steps outside and looks up at the heavy, dark clouds. A single drop, blood red, splashes at his feet, staining the rock. A second red drop falls, and then a third. He holds out his hand and another drop falls and rolls, leaving a red streak across his palm. Then another and another until his entire hand is stained red. A crack of thunder and he looks up at the sky again. Raindrops now fall on his upturned face and wash the red stain from his hand. Another crack of thunder and the rain comes down more heavily. Then it pours.

The wall of petroglyphs shines black in the downpour. They look dark and sinister now.

Rain pelts the charred cross that lies on the burnt remains of the chapel, and darkens the fresh earth over Father Marquette's grave.

In a hut in the forest, Kinta, her face now glistening with fever, tends a sick boy. She lays a wet cloth over the boy's forehead and gazes out the doorway at the pouring rain.

Atironta stands at the entrance of his longhouse looking at the puddles forming on the ground. The village looks empty but for one person scurrying for shelter.

De Clemont holds his elaborate coiffed wig in one hand and clutches a canvas tarp over his head with the other. He's soaked, shivering, and miserable. He taps one mud-caked, high-heeled, buckled shoe in the puddle at his feet.

Out on the lake, the surface of the grey water dances in the pouring rain. Two canoes slip into shore. Tonda steps out first and disappears down a portage trail to scout. The others hoist canoes and packs and follow. The rain falls in sheets but Brulé, Atsan and Savingon seem impervious to it. They move silently, sure-footed along the trail. LeCharon carries a small pack and over his shoulder the crucifix. He wraps one arm around himself trying to stay warm. His teeth chatter as he slips in the slick mud, falling behind.

The others keep a fast pace, trusting Tonda will return to warn them of any danger. The priest stumbles to keep up, his head down, shoulders stooped. He's drenched, coughing and forlorn, and a hundred yards behind.

The crucifix, which felt light when he had lifted it off the chapel wall, now digs sharply into the bones of his shoulder. It had broken his heart to watch the chapel burn — the fire of his failure. Brulé had thrown the large cross that stood in front of the chapel into the blaze. As the flames grew and crawled up the front wall of their hut, LeCharon had dashed to salvage the crucifix. He could not bear to watch Christ burn. He felt he had to return with at least that, at least the cross, as if it symbolized some sliver and vestige of dignity amidst his complete humiliation and failure. Now it is literally his cross to bear — large, heavy and sharp. Much heavier than he ever imagined possible when he decided to bring it with him.

Suddenly, LeCharon's foot slips out from beneath him. As he falls to his knees, the cross cuts into the flesh of his shoulder and a thorn from Christ's crown slices into his cheek. Staggering back onto his feet, he senses no spiritual comfort carrying the crucifix. He had thought actually travelling with it would uplift him, that it would help him somehow embrace his suffering and allow him to better offer it up to Christ. But carrying it now feels only a meaningless torment. He feels stripped, empty and alone.

Tonda returns from scouting. As he prepares another foray to scout the trail a second time, a movement catches his eye. Not forty feet away a bear, its sense of smell and hearing dulled by the rain, sniffs the air. Brulé, Atsan and Savignon had noticed the bear as well but had continued on the path. Not Tonda. He picks up a rock, moves behind the bear and pitches, deadly accurate, at the bear's rump. The bear bolts in exactly the direction Tonda had hoped.

Rounding a stand of trees, LeCharon stops, physically spent, his nerves frayed. He's heard something but no, perhaps he is imagining it. Yes, there, right in front of him — a bear, running straight towards him down the trail. LeCharon freezes, terrified. The bear bounds forward then suddenly sensing the priest, halts and lets out a roar.

Screaming in panic, the priest bolts off the path, abandoning his crucifix and pack and running as if the demons of hell snap at his heels. Tripping on his long robe, he lands hard on some rocks. But he's up again running, in great loping strides, splashing through a shallow swamp, tripping again, scrambling to his feet, racing blindly, gasping for breath, wheezing, faint, panic slowly overwhelming his senses.

He runs until he can run no more, finally collapsing. Panting in terror, he whirls around on his hands and knees, anticipating attack and certain death from the beast.

But there is no bear. He is alone. He checks left, right, once, twice. Nothing. He tries to locate himself, but it all looks the same, just trees as far as the eye can see in every direction. He realizes he is lost. The moment that thought hits him, he is hit harder by another, "They'll leave me here."

The bear sniffs the pack. Red wine from a broken flask leaks onto the ground and dissolves in the rain. The bear noses the pack and a silver cross and challis fall out.

Tonda returns once again from scouting. They stop to rest. When Savignon looks back, he notices the priest is no longer with them, "Where is LeCharon?" Brulé offers to backtrack and find him.

"Leave him," says Tonda. "He will only bring us bad luck."

"We will never get guns, Tonda, if we arrive in Québec with both priests dead." He leaves his pack hidden in the bushes, and starts a slow run back up the path as the others continue on.

Brulé soon finds LeCharon's pack and its contents. He looks at the weather-beaten crucifix and leans it up against a tree, stows the silver cross and challis in the pack and swings it over his shoulder. In the pouring rain the tracks wash away quickly, but he sees the bear's prints and the first, deep steps the priest took in the muddy trail, and heads in that direction. Shortly he stops, kneels and finds a black thread in the brambles, and then LeCharon's moccasin in the swamp.

He moves, riveted now, wholly embraced by the sentient presence of the land and the shadow traces left by the priest's frantic intrusion. He can hardly see in the fading evening light and gloom of the storm. He comes to a large, smooth rock outcrop and runs his hands over the slick, wet surface of the rock. His hand is drawn to some lichen, freshly broken and smeared into the stone. He continues to follow the trail, as if following a past presence, stitching together a seam of feeling and sense, far fainter than what the eye can see or the ear detect.

LeCharon continues to lurch through the woods in horror, his mind increasingly distraught and confused. Three large crows perched on a branch above him rend the air over and over. Their cries seem sinister, evil. He tries to cover his ears but it is no use. Finally, he pitches a rock at them. They scream in defiance as they fly off into the forest.

As he watches them his attention follows the towering trees soaring above him like vast cathedral columns or giant wraiths. He beats and pounds his arms on his legs, trunk, shoulders, trying desperately to bring some warmth to his body. He starts coughing, a piercing cough he feels deep in his lungs. His robe is torn, his arms and legs covered in bleeding cuts and deep lashes from the brambles and thorns he thrashed through in his panicked escape through the woods. Both his moccasins are gone.

Suddenly he becomes aware of new sounds, an undercurrent of soft breathing and whispered voices. At first he mistakes the sounds for those of his own wracked and heavy breathing. But no, this is something else. What is it? Where is it coming from? Trying to steady himself, to think more clearly, he slowly turns and surveys his surrounding. Then, as if out of nowhere, a face appears through the trees. A dark, ghoulish face. Distorted. Grotesque. He gasps and turns, only to confront another leering at him. Dread holds him rooted, quaking. And then he bolts, careening, bashing his way through the forest as fast as his exhausted body allows until he can go no further and stumbles to his knees, spent. As he tries to catch his breath, the forest silence is broken by the harrowing, wild howl of a wolf. He looks around in desperation. But there is no wolf. Instead, his eyes once again fall upon the girl in white just visible through the trees in the darkening forest.

"Help me," he cries, as she turns to go. "No, please, help me."

He runs towards her but just as he reaches the spot where she had stood, there is no one. He tries to collect himself, to steady his breathing, but again he hears the whispered sounds, this time even louder. He looks about, trying to locate the voice.

Then he hears it, a female voice, the same whispering voice he'd heard earlier, but clear now, "You come to me, but see nothing." LeCharon stops breathing. Then a second voice, a stern biblical voice, "Harden your hearts in the day of temptation in the wilderness." Yes, those are the words. He is not imagining this. This last one he recognizes, it is the voice of the Church. And then the softer female voice again, "Listen…I will teach you."

"Where are you?" he yells.

The biblical voice returns, "Thou shalt beat him with a rod, and shall deliver his soul from hell." Then the softer voice, "Listen…you are not alone." Voice upon voice, until LeCharon's entire rational mind dissolves. He screams and races again through the forest, falls, scrambles back on his hands and feet a few yards then finally collapses on the ground in complete exhaustion and confusion. More ghoulish faces in the trees appear before him. Trying to shelter himself from the onslaught of images and voices, he prostrates himself, pushes his body into the mud-soaked ground and buries his head under his arms. Then he hears a growl. He lifts his head. Not twenty feet away two wolves watch him. Their yellow eyes motionless in the dark. He can't breath. One lets out a long growl. In his panic LeCharon grasps something, a rock.

But, as suddenly as the wolves appeared, they're gone. And in that moment LeCharon senses something far worse approaching. Far worse.

114

This must be his end. He is sure he is about to die.

Rock in hand, he rises to his knees lifting his arm to throw, just as Brulé emerges out of the darkness and the downpour.

LeCharon falls to the ground, sobbing uncontrollably, interrupted only by a deep, hacking cough.

De Clemont pulls the remnants of his soaked, silk stocking out of the bleeding blisters on his foot. His shoe, its high-heel now missing, lay cast off in the mud. As he pries off the second shoe, the other foot reveals similar damage and blood.

"Those look awful," says de Valery. "You should have taken Petashwa's advice."

"Be quiet, will you. What am I going to do now?" He looks down the portage. One of the French aides approaches, carrying a heavy pack, his head down, soaking wet, plodding along in the pouring rain.

"Here, here," says de Clemont, trying to catch his attention. "My feet, you see…cannot walk further." The man ignores him. "Could I get you to put that pack down?" The aide plods passed without even glancing up.

"Blast you! I will see that you are flogged, you insolent dog! Do you hear me?" yells de Clemont. He pulls the oilcloth tighter around his shoulders. "Infuriating. At home all these miserable wretches would grovel. Here they behave like dumb, insolent mules." He tosses his second shoe onto the mud.

"You should try them," suggests de Valery, lifting his foot to show off one of his new moccasins. "Soaked, its true. But comfortable."

"You lose yourself, Jean-Marie. We represent the Crown. You cannot just adopt the habits of these savages. We must show them the superiority of French custom, of our culture."

"Joseph-Albert, you are being ridiculous. Just look at the superiority of your shoes. At these clothes. They represent nothing now but slow ruin," gesturing at their sodden, filthy silks and velvets.

De Clemont stung, berates the Count. "Look at your hands. They are as bad as my feet. You completely diminish our position paddling with them."

De Valery examines the blisters on his hands. "I asked Petashwa. I wanted to know. They laughed at us, you know, just sitting there idly in the canoe all day refusing to paddle."

"Let them laugh. I abhor becoming like them. These beasts. And how can you continue paddling with your hands like that?"

"Petashwa told me that the skin gets tough if I keep it up."

"Petashwa. Petashwa. You mean like a peasant. You want hands like a peasant?"

De Valery feels a flush of anger at his old friend, who becomes more foreign to him each day they are out here. He finds de Clemont's cynical disdain for everything around him exhausting. As long as he had shared his friend's disdain, he hadn't noticed. But now he's repelled by it. While the wilderness pushed de Clemont deeper into cynicism and despair, somehow it released de Valery from his. True, at this moment he feels cold, soaked from the incessant rain, miserable really, but he does feel it directly. He can't pretend it is other than it is. Or that he can change it. Blunt, plain and present. And strangely, he finds he accepts the intensity of it.

Soldiers, aides and Algonquin silently plod by with heavy packs or canoes. De Valery sees Champlain coming down the path. He carries a small pack and walks with a long cane, limping slightly as he approaches.

"This portage will be the longest of the trip. Well, until we get to the Land of the Wendat. We have one….Oh, that looks painful," says Champlain, wincing at the sight of de Clemont's blistered feet. "You should try these," pointing at his moccasins. "Did Petashwa not give you a pair?"

"He feels his represent his station better," mocks de Valery, pointing at the broken shoe in the mud."

"Well, I suppose you only make that mistake once. Must soldier on. I feel every old wound flaring up now with this wet cold," he says as he continues down the path.

De Valery feels no desire to hear De Clemont's next complaint and surprises himself by abruptly following Champlain. De Clemont stands looking at him. He feels betrayed. He seethes that his old friend has not stood by him. Now, especially, when he needs him most. He decides in that instant, staring at de Valery's back as he disappears along the portage trail, that he has finished with this expedition. He will find some way, any way to get back to France. He gazes down at his shoes, kicks one impatiently into the woods and with the help of his cane limps slowly, barefoot, after the others.

A rock overhang shelters the two men from the pouring rain. Brulé has lit a fire against a rock wall and the light and heat are welcome and bright compared to the pouring rain and sodden forest outside. It feels safe.

LeCharon lies on the ground of the dry cave, his red-rimmed eyes watching the flames. His breath rasps; his body convulses with constant coughing, as Brulé tends the fire. It wasn't easy finding anything dry enough to burn. But the fire does burn and he carefully adds larger sticks and stacks damp ones close to the heat to dry.

"The wolves," whispers LeCharon. "Did you see the wolves?"

Brulé looks at him and smiles. "You attracted strong spirit, Charon. I am impressed."

"Wolves, two wolves," trying to get Brulé to understand the danger.

"Yes, yes. I saw them. They were there to help you, not hurt you." He realizes LeCharon has no idea what he means. The wolves were messengers, the priest's personal messengers, and powerful ones, there to help him connect to what Brulé himself has come to understand as a breathing presence alive in everything. A presence the priest had utterly resisted.

The priest's idea of spirit as God the Father, a creator who does not actually remain embedded as a part of his own creation, differs dramatically to the Wendat view that that Creator remains very much present and alive in everything, animate and inanimate. And those two wolves, had he been able, could have led the priest to that understanding. But Brulé doubts the priest will ever understand or realize the great benefit they could have bestowed, or the sacred power they offered. LeCharon begins coughing again — racking coughs.

"You must get that robe off so we can dry it."

LeCharon shakes his head vigorously. Brulé leans over to help him but he resists, turning away and pulling the robe tighter around himself.

"Charon with that cough, you must get dry. You could die. I have seen it."

The priest feels the clammy, wet cloth pressed against his skin. He shivers, his teeth chattering. Brulé again tries to pull the robe over the priest's white, sickly nakedness. As he pulls the robe up over his back, he sees a lacework of thin scars from self-flagellation. He pulls the robe free of his shoulders then over his head. He jams a long stick into both sides of the cave wall and hangs the robe close to the heat of the fire to dry. LeCharon crawls closer to the warmth and curls into a tight ball.

Brulé turns to say something but the priest is already asleep. Once again he examines the lines on the priest's back, penance for some failing of faith or spirit. He pulls off his own leather vest and hangs it over the pole as well. Then he tends the fire trying to spread as much heat as possible into the overhang, hoping to keep the priest warm.

The flames flicker and leap. He picks up a piece of birch bark and cuts it carefully, then punches holes along the edges and splits a thin cedar root down its length. He sews the root into the holes, weaving and pulling them tight. Every now and then he stops to add the more sticks to the fire as his birch bark pot takes shape. He heats pine gum on a stick and seals the seams of the pot on the inside.

Finally, he ventures back out in search of wintergreen, the inner bark of the black cedar and balsam. He fills the bark pot from a puddle. Then he scours the forest for firewood, breaking off dead spruce branches thatched by the heavy growth of a live branch directly above them.

As he heads back to the overhang, the rain begins to fall more softly. He hangs the bark pot above the fire; he knows it won't burn as long as he keeps it full of water. He adds the herbs to the pot and more sticks to the fire.

LeCharon wheezes and coughs lightly from time to time, but he sleeps, exhausted. Brulé rests his back against the now warm wall of rock. He fans the fire to increase the heat while keeping as much of the smoke out of the cave as possible.

Over twenty years ago he had been in this very forest, a forest sacred to the Wendat. He marvels that of all places LeCharon could have stumbled upon, it was here — here where the Wendat performed their vision quests. Young men cleansing themselves with drumming and chanting, sweat lodges and finally in days of isolation and fasting, each one opened to the Great Mystery and to the deep spirit that surrounds us all. And each one met and united with their spirit animal. Brule's was a white hawk. He had heard the swift whisper of its flight and then, in three powerful beats of its wide, white wings it landed in front of him. That bird held him in his fierce gaze until he merged and fused with its spirit. From that moment on, the white hawk became his guardian and spirit companion.

Brulé knows this sacred place would pull a person in and strip them to their core. He wonders now, as he feels the presence of the forest play on his own mind, what trespassing here would do to a mind without ceremony, preparation and unattended by elders. He gazes at the fire, the warmth relaxes the tension in his body. Steam gently rises off the hot leather of his leggings. His mind slowly drifts, loses focus, when suddenly, he bolts upright, aware of movement just outside the cave. There, right in front of him, lit by the fire, stands a commanding soldier. His chain mail and armour gleam in the firelight.

"Father."

"You fled, Etienne."

"You know what I fled. The endless dead, and your slain, ravaged body hanging from the city wall."

"You see it approaches you here."

"I see that…now. But why does it become so inevitable, the war, the death?"

"That is not your question to answer. At least not now. You have chosen correctly. That choice creates destiny. The clearer the destiny, the less the choice. Follow whatever sliver of hope you can find…to the end."

As suddenly as he had come, he was gone.


When the priest awakens the next morning, sunlight streams and flickers through the trees. Raindrops, still hanging from the leaves, sparkle in the morning light. The woods clamor with birdsong. The forest seems rejuvenated, alive, the air fresh.

Brulé hands the dry robe to the priest, who quickly pulls it over his head and body, anxious to hide his nakedness. He starts to cough, but not as violently as the night before. Brulé hands him the bark pot from the fire.

"Drink it. It will help your cough."

LeCharon clasps the warm, bark pot with both hands, breaths in the dense, steaming herbs, and then sips the tea. They sit quietly, watching the fire. Then suddenly LeCharon starts, looking at Brulé in alarm, "The Iroquois, the fire?"

"No Iroquois would come here. They fear it. This forest is sacred to the Wendat. We call it the Forest That Speaks Only Truth. Or perhaps you did not hear."

"I did hear. She is here. With me. I will not leave this isle. If I go I may never return."

Brulé observes the priest keenly, realizing that it was not only LeCharon's body that had taken a cruel beating from this forest the night before.

"Drink. We must find the others."

LeCharon finishes the tea as Brulé prepares for them to leave. The moment they head into the woods, LeCharon gasps. Brulé turns and sees him cowering. Before him, lodged in a tree, a red face stares back, its grotesque features grimacing. He sees another. Brulé takes him by the arm and leads him over to one. He touches the wooden mask and pulls LeCharon's hand over so he can touch it.

"You saw these yesterday?"

LeCharon nods, wide-eyed, as he suddenly notices similar masks lodged in trees throughout the forest.

"Healing and vision masks," Brulé explains. He realizes how terrifying they would appear to someone in the dark, lost and alone…and here of all places. He wonders again at the chance, and destiny, that brought the priest to the very place most spiritually alive for the Wendat. The vision quest, with its terrifying visions, dramatic insights, and above all the need for surrender, requires the guidance of experienced elders and rituals. It requires preparation and fasting. Stumbling into the forest as LeCharon had, afraid, resistant, may have pushed the man too far and shown him too much.

He watches now as the priest stares from mask to mask, then up into the trees, then down to something at his feet. His attention is being pulled like that of young child, seeing things anew, fresh, alive, startling.

Gently pulling LeCharon's arm to encourage him to follow he starts to run at a slow pace through the forest. The priest shuffles along behind. Brulé knows the others will have waited at the end of the portage until he arrived and that would give them a safe vantage point down the lake to have an early warning of the arrival of Iroquois canoes. He feels certain they would have come to find him if they saw Iroquois approaching so he moves quickly through the forest. LeCharon limps along, desperate not to get left behind.

Back on the portage trail, Brulé waits for the priest to catch up. He had washed LeCharon's bleeding arms and legs the night before and rubbed the deep cuts and lashes with clay to help stop the bleeding. But they now bleed afresh. Blood runs down his calves and forearms. He cuts such a pathetic and broken figure.

Well-trodden for generations, the winding portage trail settles Brulé. Finding himself in that forest unprepared the night before had revealed to him many visions. In addition to his brief experience with his father, Nuttah had been there. And his daughter. And Kinta. His spirit animal, the White Hawk, had come to him also. But he was unprepared, so the outcome felt vague and unsettling, yet at the same time both powerful and demanding. Now back on the portage trail, feeling his feet firmly gripping the earth with each step, breath filling his lungs, he reconnects to a world more familiar, concrete and physical.

They make good time until Brulé comes to an abrupt stop. He kneels, tracing his hands over footprints. The rain has washed most of them away but they were deep. Deep from a hard, twisting wrench. On his knees now, piecing the clues together, all of a sudden the ground seems covered in deep, forced footprints. A struggle. A small group caught by a second large group, a fight, brief, and then all the footprints head back down the portage trail. The clues rapidly coalesce in his awareness, as a sense of alarm and dread engulfs him.

He leaves the trail now and runs through the woods. He's forgotten about the priest in his rising fear of what must have befallen the others and who might be waiting at the end of the portage. LeCharon finally catches up to Brulé, only to see him bolt off into the woods. The priest, terrified at once again being abandoned, stumbles along the portage trail as quickly as he can, muttering incoherently.

Brulé runs until he finally sees sky through a break in the trees ahead — the lake at the end of the portage. He slows, crouches and silently crawls towards the clearing at the shoreline. Hearing nothing unusual, he sinks still lower and moves up to the very edge of the clearing. Then he sees it. He buckles, as if someone has physically punched him in the gut. Three figures tied to trees, burnt and mutilated.

An image momentary flashes in his mind —Totiri, surrounded by flames, approaching him with the glow of a red-hot tomahawk gleaming in the night.

Brulé lets out a howl. He knows the Iroquois are gone, but he doesn't care now. If his son and Savignon are dead, he doesn't care about Iroquois, or guns. He pounds his fist on the ground.

He hears LeCharon coughing behind him, then watches as he approaches into the clearing and grasps the sight before them. The priest lets out a cry at the sight of the tortured bodies, holding his hand up to shield his eyes from the horror.

"The trumpet of judgment blows," whispers the priest.

"The trumpet of judgment," repeats Brulé to himself. "What have I done?"

Suddenly, he hears the cawing of a crow. A distinct cry, two long, a pause, one short. Brulé lifts his head, alert now. The cry repeats, two long, then the short. Brulé returns the call. And again, the bird calls out. Relief overwhelms him. He inhales deeply, able to breath again. Through the forest, on the other side of the clearing, he sees Savignon, then Atsan and Tonda.

Brulé rushes over to Atsan embracing him in a tight bear hug, as if to squeeze life back into the hollow, anguished space he had just felt inside at the thought of their death. He laughs and embraces Savignon.

"God, I thought that was you." Then he turns abruptly, "Who are they?"

"Algonquin from Québec," answers Savignon.

"What's left of them," adds Atsan.

"I recognize one of them. He is Petashwa's assistant," says Savignon.

Tonda gestures at the ground of the clearing. "Many Iroquois were here."

"Did you find anything?" asks Brulé.

"We saw where they were captured when we came down the trail. Nothing else."

"I saw that too," notes Brulé.

"The Iroquois were heading our way to attack the Wendat," Savignon concludes. "Just as we thought they would. But then they overtook these three, tortured them, then went back the way they came." He shakes his head. " I don't understand. What could they have learned from them that would make them go back?"

"With their guns they would fear nothing," says Atsan.

Tonda points at the mutilated bodies, "They were tortured for information. This is not ritual torture. Too quick."

"But why would they talk?" asks Atsan.

"These Algonquin do not live like one of us anymore, Atsan. They live in Québec, in the fort. They sleep in a bed. They eat at a table. Maybe for twenty years now. The inner armour a Wendat has to protect himself from pain, they have lost that. Once the fear of pain arises you cannot hide it. The Iroquois saw that. And, they know that for Algonquin to travel this route now, it must be a crucial mission. Whatever the Iroquois discovered here was enough for them to abandon their attack on the Wendat." Brulé paces as he speaks, looking from one dead body to the next, trying to piece together the scene and to better read its meaning.

"Petashwa knew the risk from the Iroquois this year," says Savignon. "We told him. Why would he risk this route?"

"He would not have allowed it. Nor would Champlain," adds Brulé. "And if not them, then who would have that kind of authority to make such a reckless decision? It makes no sense."

Brulé paces now and as he passes the remains of the fire in the middle of the clearing, something catches his attention and he kneels. On the edge of the fire pit, held perhaps by wet fingers before being dropped in the flames, lies a two-inch piece of paper with a perfect right angle. He studies the ashes of the fire. They had been flattened by the rain, but no one had poured a bucket of water on them, disturbing them, to put out the fire. Which meant they had probably finished their torture just as it started to rain hard. If the Iroquois had left shortly afterward, Brulé calculates they were by now close to two days away.

Brulé stands again. "They carried a letter. The Iroquois found it, could not read it, burnt it, then they tortured them to find out what it said."

"That message must have been for you," says Savignon. "Who else?"

"Petashwa would not risk this whole expedition on a piece of paper." He paces again now. "He is much too smart and crafty for that. He would not hide anything in the canoe because he knows the Iroquois would want a birch bark canoe and take it. So he must have put something…" He stops pacing and looks again at the bodies, "something on them."

Brulé stares over at the three gruesome, charred forms. He twitches and hunches down, his body reacting involuntarily to the memory these bodies provoke. Of the three, the one in the middle and on the left, stripped naked, are burnt and beaten beyond recognition. Only Petashwa's assistant remains recognizable. He hangs slumped, lashed to the tree, the top of his head bashed in, his chest and neck burnt black.

"He defied them. The other two showed their fear and the Iroquois found out what they needed. Then they clubbed him and left."

Brulé goes over to the body of the assistant. His belt hangs loose, slit. An Iroquois must have cut it to slide off the pouch in search of valuables. Brulé pulls the belt free, studies both sides, then throws it away. The man's leggings have slid down his thighs. He bends, lifts one leg of the Algonquin and pulls his left legging off. He pulls it inside out, studies it, then pitches it aside. He pulls the right legging off, and turns it inside out. "Ah"

"What is it?" asks Atsan.

"Damn you, Champlain," yells Brulé. "You damn fool!"

"What?" clamor the others.

Brulé holds up the message inked along the inside of the leather legging.

"Champlain is out here."

"But why? Why now?" asks Atsan.

"He does not come for twenty years and he chooses now." He flings the legging into the woods in a fury. "That is why the Iroquois went back. Capturing Champlain is more enticing than attacking the Wendat. That can wait. They think of ransom and more guns. A lot more guns."

"But why is he out here? He must be coming to see you," concludes Savignon.

"He only says where we are to meet them. And when. And he comes with a new Jesuit superior…but why would he be coming? None of it makes sense." He looks over at LeCharon and asks, "Du Barre. Do you know him?"

LeCharon looks up, wide-eyed, gaping. Then he gazes up at the trees. "Oh brother, what a strange path you choose for glory."

The priest's mental collapse is increasingly apparent to Brulé; the man seems unhinged, lost in some Biblical universe within himself.

"Champlain wants us to meet him four days before the full moon at the Lake of Many Bays."

"That is four days from here," offers Savignon.

"But we would not have got the message for days yet. We never would have got there in time," says Atsan.

"Champlain probably planned on making camp and resting until we arrived. He would want us with him when he meets the Wendat. But still, why risk sending these three so recklessly. And why is he here?"

Atsan points to the three bodies, "This all happened before the rain. The Iroquois will be at least a day and a half ahead of us by now. We cannot warn Champlain."

"The damn stupidity of it," curses Brulé. "Why now? Of all times. If the Iroquois catch them, that will be the end of New France. Champlain, a prisoner. And no chance for us to get guns."

The disaster that will soon overtake the French camp, and all his plans, overwhelms Brulé. He sinks to his knees as the full implication of Champlain's predicament hits home — the unraveling of his plan for guns, the deadly shifts of power to the Iroquois that will ensue, and with the English too, and perhaps the fall of Québec...as well as the hopelessness of defending the Wendat.

As the devastation unfolds, layer by layer, in Brulé's mind, LeCharon standing alone in the clearing, lifts up his arms, as if to petition the trees. "Whose thought is this and from whence does it come? Within me? Is this God's work?" His voice gains power as his raving intensifies. He holds his head high, preaching now to the forest. But as mad as his words sound, the clarity with which they are uttered and the power of his speech, starts to draw Brulé back to the moment.

"I watch it," continues LeCharon to the trees, "I am its witness. We are but puppets before the Lord. Behold, 'tis all rehearsed here before the

Fall. Yet we are lifted up out of this smoke and flame unto our Glory."

"One priest dead," says Savignon, "the other mad."

Brulé suddenly looks up at Atsan, then Savignon and scrambles to his feet. "The fall, the falls," he says, "Smoke River. A day on foot. We could go down the rapids. Below the falls, the portage leads to the Lake of Many Bays. We could be there before the Iroquois."

Tonda raises his hands as if to ward off a blow or spell as Savignon, too, rejects the idea, "No one has ever gone down those falls. They are cursed."

"Achak did," corrects Brulé.

"That is a legend," says Atsan. "He is a spirit, not a man."

"A panther lives in that water, " explains Tonda. "You will hear her laugh as she pulls you under. She will hold you. You will never join the ancestors. No man will be allowed to pass."

"Can she take us all?" asks Brulé.

"Fear the panther, White Hawk," warns Tonda. "More than you fear Iroquois. I think you do not understand the price you would pay."

Brulé recognizes their fear, but the very moment the idea of the falls came to him, the string of disasters that had been unfolding in his mind, if the Iroquois capture Champlain, suddenly stopped. He now sees a way forward and with a brute resolve, he ignores everything else.

"Where are the canoes?" he asks.

Savignon points and Brulé bolts across the clearing through the trees to where they are hidden. He shoulders one and starts back across the clearing and up the trail. As he passes Atsan, he warns, "Keep the priest safe."

Three Wendat stand in confusion looking at one another. "He will

130

need someone to cut the trail. He cannot get a canoe there alone," says Savignon.

Tonda lifts his hand and shakes his head, trying to dissuade Savignon. But Savignon's fear wrestles with his loyalty to Brulé. He cowers at the misery that would fill his existence after death with no Wendat, no ancestors, just the torment of this vicious sorcerer, the panther, to torment him. But as he watches Brulé run up the trail with the canoe, the moment he disappears from view, Savignon knows he must follow. He too now crosses the clearing, selects a pack, and without looking back at the others for fear they'll argue him out of his madness, hurries up the trail in pursuit of his friend.

Atsan knows as Savignon races across the clearing that he too will follow. He hurries to catch up, hauling the other canoe onto his shoulders. He yells over at LeCharon, "You must follow me. If I leave you with him," nodding at Tonda, "he will kill you."

His words fail to register with LeCharon. The priest gazes past Atsan, "Fear not death in a world of blind and vicious men." Atsan, frustrated at the priest's resistance, points at the three mutilated bodies and then at Tonda. "He will do that to you if you stay with him alone." The image finally seems to break through LeCharon's jumbled mind and he grips Atsan's arm. "Follow me," and he starts up the path with the second canoe, the priest close behind.

Tonda left alone in the clearing, bellows in frustration and throws his tomahawk; it spins across the clearing striking deep into a tree.

Savignon, with a tomahawk in each hand, cuts a trail through the forest. He works fast, cutting each branch as close to the trunk as he can so no sharp ends could puncture the fragile bark canoe. Brulé and

Atsan come after him, with LeCharon limping behind, but determined to keep up.

Resting only long enough to take turns cutting the trail and carrying the canoes, they continue for hours until the light begins to fade. The dense forest gives way onto a flat outcrop of rock. Exhausted, Brulé finally hoists the canoe from his shoulders, sets it on the ground, and feels his legs buckle beneath him. Every muscle and joint aches and burns. On his hands and knees he slowly lifts his head to survey the valley that stretches out below them.

The forest drops down steeply to a river that cuts a steep canyon through a wall of rock. The wall rises up out of the forest, creating a long impassable barrier that snakes back up through the valley beyond their outcrop. The only way past that barrier lies on the river through the canyon. This is the Smoke River.

"You can hear the rapids," says Brulé, pointing to the mist rising up from the rock canyon far below. The others, collapsed on the ground, are too tired to even look.

"That sounds like falls, not rapids," groans Savignon.

Brulé ignores the comment. "We will rest here tonight and we can be at the river in the morning."

"And dead by midday," is Savignon's bleak response.

"Savignon, if we get there, and save Champlain…and the new Jesuit, they will give us guns. They will." He's been letting this line of thinking inspire him all day. "We should have a fire. It will warm us, inside and out."

As they build the fire, the dark closes in. They sit watching the flames, each deep in his own thoughts. Both Brulé and Atsan lace and tie long thin spruce roots to the gunwales of the canoes, creating a lattice grid over the bow.

Savignon breaks the silence, "Do you think if we save Champlain, he might send me to France?"

"To visit?" asks Brulé. Savignon nods. "Not to live?" he inquires further.

"No, not to live," answers Savignon. "Just to see it again. I was so young. So innocent, naive. I need to see it again, now. See for myself what you and Champlain have told me. The rot, the decay. How many people suffer and die to allow that court to live as they do. I never saw that. I just saw a place of magic. If I did go, and could see it for what it is, it would break the spell. I want to be here, Etienne. I know that. I just need to bury a longing that still remains with me."

"And Anne-Marie?"

"That is foolish, I know. She married. She has children. I need to bury that longing too. I am Wendat. And I live as a Wendat. For the Wendat. That is clear."

"Well, yes, I think you are right. You should see it. See the court now. See the hoards of poor, taxed wretches that feed the court with their blood. Some day those masses of poor will say, 'enough'."


When they wake at first light, Tonda is sitting in the clearing. He hasn't slept. "If I went back to the village alone, what could I say? To my people. I know my spirit-bear would be ashamed of me. If I abandon you, he would leave me. But I have sat here since the moon was there," pointing up at the sky, "and listened to the water below and I need to warn you what this panther will do."

"Tonda," Savignon says harshly in a flash of anger, "You have been called here. By spirit, by shame. It does not matter. We are here now for one thing." He had always been terrified of Tonda and he's surprised by his own outburst. And Tonda, always dismissive of Savignon, of what he perceived as his lack of courage and skill, flushes with anger and shame.

Atsan had glimpsed this fear when he asked Tonda about the trip to the Iroquois. But he had never seen the war chief like this. His fearlessness and ferocious cunning fighting Iroquois were legend. So his fear now, both repels him, and cracks his own tenuous resolve. He wonders if Tonda isn't right. Atsan begins to succumb to his own fear, unnerved. But Brulé remains undaunted. "Tonda, like you I cannot go back to the village. We are the hope of the Wendat. Here. Come. We will face this now, together."

Brulé swings a canoe onto his shoulders, and Savignon, tomahawks in hand, begins cutting a path down to the river far below.

Standing by the water's edge, De Valery gazes out across the lake. The sunlight has begun cutting through the dense clouds casting shifting and dramatic patterns of light and shadow over the hills. Tight up against the shore a thin line of sunlight turns the water a rich, deep ultramarine after days of sullen grey. He feels happy here, just standing with the warmth of the sun on his face. He cannot remember the last time such a simple thing affected him so deeply.

His quiet reverie is suddenly broken by an outburst of coarse laughter. He looks over to see De Clemont standing with three soldiers. As he speaks the soldiers lean in close to hear. De Valery finds the idea of de Clemont sharing anything with these tough, hardened characters odd. De Clemont still pieces together his court attire, the once ravishing, matching colors, their sheen and sparkle reduced now to a torn, lifeless grey. He still wears his long wig but the rich curls hang like dead fur against the peeling skin of his sunburnt face. De Valery himself had abandoned his European shoes early on; their impractically was obvious. Then piece by piece he'd also abandoned the elaborately shaped pantaloons, the velvet jacket and his wig, after witnessing their deteriorated state on de Clemont. The entire dress code had proved ludicrous in this wilderness; he certainly was willing to admit that now. But de Clemont clung stubbornly to the inanity of it all.

A loon suddenly breaks the calm surface of the lake, piercing the air with its wild, mournful call. Immediately one of the soldiers picks up his musket, aims and fires; the musket ball slaps the water and the loon dives. De Clemont claps the man on the back and jeers with the other two soldiers at his missed shot. De Valery finds his interaction with these soldiers very peculiar. So out of keeping.

The loon resurfaces again not far away. The other two soldiers quickly shoulder their muskets and fire, shrouding themselves in a cloud of smoke. One ball hits the water. The other hits the loon. It flaps for a few seconds, its wings thrashing the water frantically and then is still, its body lifeless. The soldiers cheer as de Clemont pulls out a coin from his purse and flips it to the soldier who has successfully killed the bird.

De Valery's mood of contentment quickly dissipates, as he stares at the loon's dead body floating on the water. He hates the mindless sport and the boisterous clowning of de Clemont and the three soldiers. His eyes meet Petashwa's who stands not far away. He recognizes a mutual incomprehension and sadness reflected in the Algonquin's eyes.

Brulé hacks at several branches. As they fall away, he steps out onto the smooth rock by the river's edge. They had followed a long, vertical ridge down from their campsite, hoping to find a way over the barrier and thus avoid the rapids. But the wall proved impassable and in the end has led them to the river's edge. Their only way forward now is down the river that moves swiftly in front of them before disappearing into a deep, sheer-walled canyon. The roar of the water, which they have heard all morning, rages, pounding and shaking the ground. Heavy mist from the falls and rapids settles on them like a gentle rain.

Confronted now with a hint of the power that lies just beyond their sight, Brulé feels his resolve falter. He looks at the others; they too look out, cowering at what awaits them downriver. For Brulé, this feels like certain death, but for the Wendat it is even more. The panther terrifies them more than the sheer power and menace of the river, even more that death itself.

Atsan yells something but Brulé can't hear him over the roar of the river. Thoughts race through his mind. They could still return back up the way they came. They could return to their village. Or go and see what the Iroquois have done to Champlain. He could travel deeper into the woods, live with one of the trader tribes he has met, far from the Iroquois and their guns. He could penetrate deeper into the country he loves. He could still escape.

Out of nowhere, however, his father's words of warning come back to him: "Follow whatever sliver of hope you find…to the end". A new resolve grips him. He knows only he will get in a canoe and start down this river. With his tomahawk he cuts spruce boughs and weaves them into the root lattice he had tied over the bow of the canoe the night before. When finished it creates a thatched cover over the front of the canoe to repel water that will inevitably gush over the bow once in the rapids. He then carries the canoe to the edge of the river and slips it into the quiet eddy of water by the shore. Just three feet away the current flows dark and fast down into the canyon. He grabs his pack and lashes it into the canoe. He steps into the stern, settles on his knees, paddle in hand. Finally, he dares to look up at Savignon.

Until that moment Savignon had no intention of getting in a canoe. He had thought that, surely, now they were here, the raging thunder of the river literally shaking the ground they stood on, that this would be evidence enough of the clear insanity of their plan. Even while watching Brulé place the canoe in the water and even when he got in, nothing had registered. It was the look in Brulé's eyes that broke the spell. It was the look that shocked him.

Standing there on the river's edge he had wanted to run. Or hide. Somewhere. Anywhere. But that look had cut through everything and spoke to the years, over twenty years, this man had stood by him. How he had helped him reenter his life with the Wendat after his upheaval in France. How he had embraced his people, the Wendat. And how he was embracing his people now. Right here. He was doing this for them, for the Wendat. Savignon takes a step forward, and then another, as he realizes that, yes, he will join him. He will get in the canoe.

As Savignon settles in the canoe, kneeling in the bow, Tonda approaches Brulé, yelling over the roar of the river. "She will hold you down. You will never escape her grip." He holds Brulé's arm, clearly hoping to reason him out of his suicidal decision. "Your spirit will be hers forever. It is no way for a man to die." The reality of the panther now claws at Tonda's heart. But Brulé shakes him off. He points first to himself, then down the river. Tonda leans in close to him again, "We should sacrifice the black robe to the panther now. They are both sorcerers. Maybe she will take him."

But Brulé turns to LeCharon and motions to him. The priest quickly shuffles over, as Brulé readjusts the pack to make room. As he steps into the canoe, Brulé forces him to crouch low, his head to his knees. "When we start down the river," he yells over the noise, "no matter what happens, stay there, like that. Keep your head down." Immediately the priest sits up, raises his arms. "Who beats this heart and raises this hand? Who guides us? It is vast, indifferent, horrible," he calls out to no one in particular.

Atsan, seeing his father, then Savignon, and finally the priest step into the canoe, knows he must join them. He knows but not because he decides. He knows because his feet now tell him as he walks back to the woods to cut boughs to thatch the bow of his canoe. He returns with an armful, and quickly, expertly, weaves the bow cover as Brulé had done. Then he carries his canoe to the water's edge. Tonda holds him by the arm, but he pulls free and slips the canoe into the water alongside the other one. He carries the other pack down, lashes it into the canoe and gets into the bow. Now in the canoe seeing the water racing into the steep-walled gorge, he panics. But he knows he will not back down.

He turns to Tonda, alone and immobile on the rock. Tonda stares first at them, then down at the river, up the path and finally raising his head he howls at the sky, his arms outstretched, his fists clenched. His anger and frustration spent, he picks up the last paddle and gets in the stern of the canoe behind Atsan.

Brulé leans forward to LeCharon and yells, "I do not care who or what you pray to Charon. But pray to something and do it now."

All but LeCharon take tobacco from their pouches and, chanting to the spirit of the river, throw a handful into the water. They perform the same ritual for the panther. Brulé had early on embraced the Wendat connection to spirit and has ever since never failed to follow the prescriptions carefully. But now, with the resounding rampage thundering below them, the act of throwing tobacco and calling out to the river, feels futile. He again pushes LeCharon's head down low onto the floor of the canoe.

He glances over at Atsan beside him in the other canoe, leans forward, taps Savignon with the end of his paddle and then they both dig in. In just two swift strokes the current catches them and the smooth black water sucks them forward in its grip. The canyon rises quickly into a narrow, black gorge. For fifty yards they feel the current pulling them faster and faster.

Brulé thinks to look back to see if Atsan and Tonda are following but at just that moment the swift, smooth current buckles and drops and he and Savignon face a white torrent of water churning between both sides of the towering gorge. Despite their growing speed, they must steer their path down the river carefully. Rocks, both hidden and visible, leap into view on the left, then on the right, now in the middle. Brulé and Savignon pull and pry the canoe left and right carving and cutting a path away from the rocks. They look to stay in the narrow channel of smooth, fast water, the chute, as much as possible and away from the turbulent chaos in and around the boulders. They scout for and cleave to the chute, yet at the bottom of each chute a standing wave awaits, rising straight up and curling back towards them. The vertical walls on each side enclose the current, press it, rush it, so they find no relief, no quiet eddies to pull into.

Savignon sees a submerged boulder and drives his paddle deep down beside the bow of the canoe. He pries hard; the canoe leaps left just as the massive, pale leviathan looms up beside them and then disappears. But the move hurls them across the river toward the sheer wall of the gorge. They pry hard, hewing away and then away again from another huge boulder in their path. They speed past the rock, paddling hard to avoid the ripping mayhem of churning chaos below the rock.

The canoe heaves up, down and then shoots across black water and again drops down a smooth black chute. They claw their way out to one side of the standing wave at the bottom of the chute, pull hard to avoid rocks looming on their right, swinging immediately down another chute before careening out one side into a taut mass of swift, black water. Huge rocks jut up left and right and they pry and pull and lever a path around them. Brulé and Savignon move and respond together as one, the canoe responding crisply and immediately to their practiced skill. But the river is relentless. The rock walls box them in tight. Touch the wall but once and the bark canoe would shred and disintegrate.

Down another chute and then they bounce madly through sets of dancing waves coming at them head on and from the left and right off the canyon walls. Despite the thatched cover, water pours over the bow into the canoe. They must get it out. The water weighs the canoe down, making it sluggish to manoeuvre, its nimbleness gone. As the canoe heaves, they struggle to keep upright and not capsize.

Just then, Brulé sees a break in the rock face ahead on the right. They steer toward it, narrowly missing a huge boulder. As soon as they pass it, they face a boiling mass of white water heading off to the left and down the river. But to the right, a narrow, black pool of still water appears. They drive the canoe, clawing desperately with their paddles for purchase against the massive current and the sodden weight of their own canoe and kiss the edge of the quiet water, carve in and glide across the smooth, dark pool and come to rest against the rock wall.

Brulé nudges LeCharon, still crouched low, head down, in the middle of the canoe and he slowly sits up. The sheer walls soar fifty feet above them on each side. Two long escarpment walls plunging down one side of the river join here, creating this quiet pool — the thundering chaos of the main current only a few feet away. While the roar of water and heavy mist and spray continue to engulf them, still for the moment they are safe.

Brulé retrieves a bowl from the pack and starts bailing water out of the canoe. But his attention rests on the top of the chute above them, looking for Atsan and Tonda, either in their canoe or out of it. He bails quickly in case he needs to somehow help them to safety, but he knows if they are swept out past him in the boiling madness, he could do nothing more than watch.

Just then the second canoe pops into view as it pitches down the chute toward them and slices into the quiet eddy coming to rest beside them. Atsan lets out a yell of relief, barely audible in the thundering roar that surrounds them. Their canoe, too, heaves and sloshes with the weight of water they've taken in.

The relentless, exhilarating battle against the massive bullying power of the river strips them of their fear of the panther. The river itself now completely consumes their awareness. It provokes, taunts and mocks them. Its tyrannical power assaults and besieges their skill, their strength, their will. But they have survived. Their spirits soar. They feel elated, exuding confidence and hope once again.

They bail until the canoes are empty. Then stretch, breath, readjust the packs, readying themselves for what awaits below. They yell to each other, trying to communicate but the roar of the rapids pounds and reverberates up the walls of rock, drowning out their voices. Conversation is impossible. Brulé motions, he's ready to go. He pushes LeCharon back to the bottom of the canoe and they turn it around in the quiet of the eddy to face the current. The canyon wall extends out past them, hiding the view of what lies ahead. Brulé rests his hand briefly on the shoulder of both Atsan and Tonda as he passes them, then he and Savignon drive their paddles through the smooth water and shoot into the crashing current. As they hit it, they are whipped downstream. Pivoting they immediately hug one side of another chute that funnels down into a massive wave curling backwards towards them. They slice out past it on one side as the waves buck and kick at the canoe.

With the canoe empty of water they are able to regain their line of attack. But then the river drops away into another huge, steep chute, and the wave at the bottom engulfs the bow of the canoe. Water pours over the thatched cover. They drive their way up and over the wave and down its back, then up the wave beyond it. Each wave torques them left, then right. Brulé and Savignon fight to stay upright as the river bucks and surges. It arcs and dives and leaps like a live animal. Where they head now, the river alone decrees.

Against the wild onslaught, they fight, desperate to at least keep the canoe pointing downstream in line with the current. They're at the river's mercy. No line better than another in the wide, foaming torrent that surrounds them. They dive down through a churning white mass of foam, then released, explode up facing the black sides of the canyon. Down again into a sea of white and another surge up, the black walls looming above them. Thrust up, sucked down. Over and over, the river holds them in its frenzied grip. They fight desperately to stay upright and afloat, the canoe heaving again with the weight of the water they have taken in.

They hurtle out of the seething, cascading foam into a swift black stretch of smooth water. The gorge closes in tighter on both sides. The canyon walls close in propelling the canoe faster and faster. They can feel the angle of the river drop, steeper. And steeper. The vertical ramparts of rock squeeze tighter. The canoe charges down a cascading funnel,

a narrow chute dropping fifteen feet. At the bottom a massive white wall of water curls back towards them, its clutches ready to engulf and crush them. Brulé, in one last effort, drives his paddle in deep, holding it, holding it, pulling the canoe around, pulling it so just as they crash into the bottom of the chute they are sliding sideways. The canoe smashes against the massive standing wave and rolls, narrowly escaping being ripped in half by the force of the water folding and crashing over its length.

All sense of up or down, left or right is obliterated. Brulé is torn, pulled, buffeted, smashed by the fury of the water. He's hurled up, sucked down, pounded against rocks along the bottom, churned up and spat out. A deep laugh, harsh and maniacal, fills his ears as he pitches helplessly through the punishing, brutal barrage. He keeps hitting something, bouncing off it, something soft, but he can't understand what it is. His lungs rage for air, and then he realizes he's surrounded by sunlight for an instant, racing over smooth water. He's at the top of a waterfall and going over. He's falling. He's falling and LeCharon bolts through his awareness as he hits the explosive fury of the roiling mass of water under the falls. His body feels like it's being ripped apart in several directions at once, flung down savagely against the bottom of the river, smashed against the rocks, then sucked up toward the light, then rammed to the bottom hard.

The mocking roar of the panther's laughter fills his ears, abusive, gripping him, clutching him, pulling him to her. He bounces again against something soft as he's thrown violently back up into the light. This time as he's rammed back to the bottom, his feet hit first and he pushes off to one side. He's churned, pulled up and thrown back down. But the turmoil is less. He gets a sense of his bearings and as he hits bottom he pushes off in the same direction. The next time he hits bottom with one more push, he feels the churning calm, and it's gone. The laughter of the panther falls away. His lungs scream for air as his head bursts through the surface of the water.

He gasps for breath as he looks around. The falls drop thirty feet in front of him. His hand holds something. Clutched in a spasm of tension, his hand grips the collar of LeCharon's robe, the priest on his knees in the water beside him, coughing and hacking, fighting to get his breath back. Brulé looks desperately for Savignon. The undertow had sucked them down several times before Brulé found his feet on the bottom for just an instant to push out of its grip. Otherwise, they would still be in there beneath the falls.

He stands, slogs through the knee-deep water at the edge of the pool. Mists and spray obscure his view. Below the falls, the walls of the gorge spread out and pools and eddies form on both sides of the river. He scans the water and sees Savignon, floating face down on the far side slowly swinging back into the whirlpool where he would be sucked back down again beneath the falls. He looks desperately for some way to get to him.

Not ten feet away, a log leans against the wall of the gorge. Before his thought has caught up with his actions he heaves against the log's weight, pushing it up, up until it tilts over and falls out into the river straight towards the waterfall. He leaps onto it, the log buoying his weight. It shoots straight into the falls but being too long to get sucked under, it pitches wildly, then pivots, swinging Brulé over to the other side of the river.

The moment he sees he's free of the falls, he pushes off and swims hard to the far shore. His feet bounce along the bottom, he stumbles to get his footing in the fast current, then he's into shallow water and racing back up the shore. Savignon, still face down, drifts in an arc back towards the undertow of the falls. Brulé scrambles to the rock face behind the waterfall, dives in pushing off the rock wall towards Savignon. He snatches at Savignon's legging as his feet touch bottom. He hunches low, grinds his feet into the stones, clutches for rock with his free hand, and digs against the current trying to pull Savignon back into the undertow. He claws toward shore, Savignon tight in his grip. Then his feet have purchase on the bottom and he hauls himself and Savignon into shallow water.

Brulé grasps Savignon in a tight grip of loss and despair. Why had he done this? Why had he made this mad decision to come down the river? He is besieged with guilt and anger, anger at himself, at the river, at the guns, at the Iroquois, and the English. He's on his knees in the water and the violence of his embrace and his awkward angle pushes hard into Savignon's belly. Savignon suddenly retches a stream of water down Brulé's back. He hacks and heaves, pushing away from Brulé to get air into his lungs. Savignon's revival breaks Brulé's attention — Atsan!

He stands, scanning the falls. Tonda, he sees now, kneels in the shallow water on the far side. Spent but alive. But Atsan, where is he? He sees no sign of him. He slogs back into the water trying to see into the pounding foam and mist at the base of the falls. He can't think what to do. Should he dive below the falls? He pushes deeper into the water looking for his son in the churning foam. He stumbles and loses his balance. The current sucks at him, as he dives and crouches, grinding his feet into the gravel and rocks and clawing his way against the pull of the undertow back into shallow water. As he turns to look again at the river he sees Atsan. Fifty feet downstream his son wades up the river through a quiet eddy waving his arms to get his father's attention. Behind him a canoe floats in the shallow, quiet water of the eddy. Brulé throws his arms to the sky in relief and yells, the sound lost over the roar of the falls. Savignon has crawled further out of the water and lies on his side still heaving and retching. Tonda sits on the far shore looking at the falls, the priest beside him.

An hour later on a wide, smooth rock a hundred yards further down the river, they regroup. The walls of the gorge below the falls open into a broad canyon. The current, still swift, flows flat and smooth. They had found three of their five paddles and their second canoe, well below the falls, ripped apart and flattened, lodged between rocks, the leather pack still lashed into the wreckage.

They sit close to a fire to warm themselves. With what they are able to scavenge, they repair their one damaged, but surviving canoe. Brulé scrapes pine tar from the ruined canoe as Tonda stitches a bark patch to the gunnel of the salvaged one with a long, slender pine root. Heating the tar, Brulé smooths it with a heated rock over another patch.

Withdrawn, Tonda has said nothing for some time. Now he looks up, "Did you hear her laughter? She is evil that one. I could feel her claws gripping me. Pulling me down." He's still clearly shaken.

Savignon, stretched out on a nearby rock, also struggles to come to terms with how very close he'd been to death. "I was hers. I fought, but she had me. Screaming, taunting." He shivers.

"I thought I had lost you, my friend," says Brulé.

Tonda looks at Brulé, "You were fearless in the face of our dread and yet somehow we are all still here."

"Tonda, my connection to Wendat spirit, cannot run as deeply as it does in you," offers Brulé, as he runs his hands over the smooth patch. "Yours was a different fear to mine. And Atsan, you missed her completely."

"I could hear her laughter through the rapids," says Atsan. "But was free of her in the falls." He had by chance arrived at the top of the falls at the same moment as his capsized canoe. He had slid on top of it and in a graceless, slippery leap had jumped just far enough to be clear of the undertow below.

Brulé looks up at the sun. "The river runs flat from here. I have come upriver from the other direction to the portage into the Lake of Many Bays. It cannot be far. We could, I think, still be in Champlain's camp by night fall."

"The Iroquois could be there already," warns Savignon.

Atsan has spread all their supplies from the packs out on the rocks. All five of them and their supplies must now fit in the one canoe. He lifts the two leather satchels of gold coins to hand to Brulé. Tonda, closer, takes them to pass them on, but is surprised at the weight. He looks inside, pulling out several coins. He has seen them before but never so many.

"It is what white men do," explains Brulé. "They save gold. For years I have wondered why I still do it. What it was for. Until now."

They load the canoe and push off down the river. The rock walls soon open out and give way to forest. The canoe rides low in the smooth, fast water, slowly leaking despite their patchwork. They paddle hard and in less than two hours begin to scan the shore for the portage trail.

"There it is," says Savignon and they pull into shore.

"It is a long, hard portage," says Brulé, "but it leads to the Lake of Many Bays."

Brulé shoulders the canoe and starts up the trail. The others grab packs and paddles, racing after him. Atsan grips LeCharon by the sleeve, forcing him to keep up. The portage ascends away from the river. Now, despite their exhaustion, they must reclimb the vertical drop they have descended, both the long, steep hike all morning down from their campsite of the night before to the river, plus the drop in the steep descent of the length of the river itself.

Tonda relieves Brulé, taking the canoe from him as they keep climbing. They set a grueling pace, Atsan prodding and pulling LeCharon to ensure he keeps apace, the priest cursing with every step.

The steep trail levels out and disappears into a swamp of thick cattails. Knee-deep water over thick mud oozes and sucks at their feet. They plod through hauling their feet free with each step until they are out the other side where the trail ascends yet more steeply up through the trees. LeCharon stumbles and lurches through the swamp. He finally staggers the last few steps out onto the trail and collapses.

"Oblivious and driven madmen," mutters the priest.

Atsan yells up to Brulé, who drops his pack and quickly races back down the trail. He looks at the pitiful, broken figure of LeCharon and in one deft movement slings the priest over his shoulder and starts back up the path.

The trail becomes steeper yet through the trees. Their pace is punishing. Atsan now takes the lead, scrambling on his hands and feet up steep outcrops of rock and over boulders, pulling his way using the trees to help himself against the weight of his pack. He climbs over yet more rocks, hoists his body up and finds himself looking down a long slope of land. He yells to the others, "I see the lake!"

Savignon helps Tonda heave and steer the canoe through the trees and rocks up the last sheer pitch. Brulé's legs scream with the strain of the priest's weight on his back. He staggers up the last steep steps to the top and then rolls LeCharon onto the ground. He takes Savignon's pack, nods to him to take the priest and runs after Atsan. Spread out below them the Lake of Many Bays gleams through the trees in the afternoon sun.

Savignon prods LeCharon to his feet. The priest raises his arms to heaven petitioning for some kind of mercy. As he begins to sag, Savignon leans into him, throws him over his shoulder and lurches down the trail after the others.

They race down the long slope. The glint of sunlight on the lake shimmers from time to time through the trees, until one by one they arrive and fall exhausted in the clearing at the edge of the lake.

Savignon arrives last, staggering the final steps to the shore, where he drops LeCharon next to the others. The priest stares dull-eyed out at the water. The others scan the lake carefully. Forest surrounds it except for several outcroppings of grey rock. A mile away on the far side a hundred and fifty foot outcrop juts straight out of the water.

Brulé turns to LeCharon. "This is the Lake of Many Bays. And there is Champlain's camp. We have made it."

LeCharon squinting out over the lake, fails to see anything. Confused, he turns to Brulé, who points to one side of the high outcrop on the far shore. "There." Still, the priest fails to see the camp. "You can smell it," says Brulé. "The cook fires. And listen, chopping….And there, the

Iroquois."

"We have beaten them." says Atsan.

LeCharon grips Brulé's arm in alarm at the mention of the Iroquois.

"You see those glints of light way down there on the lake," explains Brulé. "Those are their paddles catching the sunlight."

Tonda looks up at the late afternoon light, judging how far the Iroquois must still come. "They will not attack today. By the time they paddle to this end of the lake it will be getting dark. They will wait until morning."

"The Iroquois have no reason to think Champlain will try and escape tonight," says Brulé. "If we move the camp after dark, back up this portage and onto the Smoke River, we could escape or at least defend ourselves there. We should go."

Part 3

The French make camp on a long, thin point of land jutting out into the Lake of Many Bays. Soldiers cut straight, pine saplings, dig trenches where they can and lash the pine poles to trees where they can't. The palisade will, when finished, cross and enclose the point of land from one side to the other. They leave a three-foot opening at one end of it between the palisade and the shore to serve as a gate. The Algonquin, along with a few French aides, set up tents, collect firewood and set kettles on the fire to begin the evening meal.

The priest Du Barre kneels performing Mass alone. The nobles' table has been set, but sits empty, looking as incongruous as ever in the wilderness. De Clemont stands, huddled with three soldiers, but after a few minutes, joins de Valery as he watches Champlain quietly plotting his calculations on a map spread out before him. Champlain looks up as de Clemont arrives. He no longer rises, or even thinks of it, such court protocols now long gone.

"We get the idea," says de Clemont. "Lakes and forests. Then more lakes and forests. I am ready to go home."

"We have pushed hard, I admit. But now we will rest. We can hunt for meat. Brulé should be here in a few days. When he arrives, he will lead us to the Land of the Wendat. Introduce us. The land there is different. You will see. Open, with meadows and small rivers and lakes."

"At this rate we may not get back to Québec before the ships leave for the winter."

"That is possible," admits Champlain.

"No, that is not possible!" counters de Clemont. "I plan to get back to Québec." He looks over his shoulder to see where du Barre is and if anyone can overhear them, then adds, " I intend to go back now, back to France."

"Now," exclaims de Valery. "But…how?"

"I have been busy. I have made friends with three of du Barre's soldiers. They too have had enough. We plan to head back tomorrow. I have guaranteed to protect them against charges of desertion. And I intend to pay them lavishly when we get back to France."

"Tomorrow? You play a game far more dangerous than you imagine," cautions Champlain.

"I know what he stands to gain with this expedition," motioning towards du Barre. "Richelieu said he would make sure he gets to Rome. Du Barre is rabid," explains de Clemont. "I thought you two might be interested in joining me. Certainly you, Jean-Marie. And I know this whole journey must vex you, Monsieur Champlain."

Their conversation is abruptly interrupted as two men standing on the shore of the lake call to Champlain, beckoning him to come. He looks over, relieved to have an excuse to interrupt de Clemont's treasonous

160

thoughts. Champlain excuses himself from the nobles and approaches the two men. The nobles follow.

The remains of a ten-foot wooden cross lie decomposed on the shore, its shape now only defined by the moss reclaiming it.

"How strange," says de Valery. "What is it doing here?"

"We passed through this lake twenty-five years ago," explains Champlain. "This was the biggest lake we had been on and the point had such a commanding view of the whole vista it seemed ideal. We claimed it all in the name of France. A symbol of our possession."

The cross engrosses Champlain. He remembers so vividly being out here with Brulé so many years ago. How much he had enjoyed the wide, open simplicity of living in the wilderness. To really understand and appreciate New France, he felt he should come out every two or three years. That at any rate is what he told himself at the time. But he never did again. All the relentless details of building a colony and raising interest and money in France, had engulfed him. The cross was but a decaying reminder.

Yes, this expedition itself seemed a wild fantasy. And he ached at the thought of what was, no doubt, unfolding in Québec without him. He knew he was being replaced. Richelieu had insisted on his coming with the expedition, so the Crown could install someone new without interference. With his responsibilities lifted, he realized his role in Québec was probably over.

In the first days of the expedition, he naturally assumed a leadership role, only to find du Barre frustrate and override him time and again, humiliate him really, until he had let it go and released himself from any commanding role. And slowly he'd found he enjoyed it. With time to reflect, he realized he wasn't actually unhappy now at all. Frustrated with du Barre certainly, but not unhappy. Perhaps when they returned he could move up river to Trois Rivières and help establish a new fort and leave behind all the vexing administrative duties as Governor.

"Well, the cross certainly does not look very convincing now," mutters de Clemont.

Pulled from his musings, Champlain counters, "We will put up another while we are here."

De Clemont motions for Champlain and de Valery to come closer. Champlain can feel the conspiracy brewing; his eyes meet de Valery's, who also wants no part of it. De Valery has experienced moments here that truly astonished him. He has changed. Yes, he would love to be in France. Yes, he would love to be more comfortable. But he also knows that to rebel and break company could mean prison. Or, at the least, something unimaginably worse than this. He has watched de Clemont slowly let his demons get the better of him and has made a point of spending less and less time with him. He knows that de Clemont somehow imagines that if only he could get home, his parents or court friends would have the power to save him.

De Clemont tries to gather their attention but just as he is about to speak again his opportunity is foiled. A sentry calls, pointing out to a single canoe heading straight towards them across the lake.

A hundred yards from shore, the canoe rides low in the water, barely afloat. Three men paddle while another bails water furiously. Everyone in camp turns to stare at their approach. Except for sighting a couple of Algonquin fishing camps in their first week out of Québec, they have seen no one in over three weeks.

As they near the camp, Brulé sees Champlain head towards the landing where the canoes lie along the shore. Two men follow. Even from this far away, Brulé recognizes their awkwardness; they do not seem to belong here, one in particular. He also notices soldiers, and aides and Algonquin, and on the far side of the camp, the priest.

He'd been elated since seeing the Iroquois far down the lake and realizing they have beaten them to Champlain's camp. Since the idea to go down the Smoke River had initially come to him two days ago, all his thinking had been about beating the Iroquois here. And in arriving first, with his news of the Iroquois, he felt his escape plan would guarantee Champlain's gratitude, and the assurance of guns for the Wendat. He knew it. Even the oddness of the Jesuit superior being out here now seemed a blessing for he, too, would see the dire need of guns for the Wendat.

When they had first found the tortured Algonquin, the pressing question had been why Champlain was out here at all considering the warnings the Wendat had given about the Iroquois earlier in the summer. And why they had risked the three Algonquin in the mad urgency of, what seemed, a suicide mission. Yet once the idea had hatched to reach Champlain before the Iroquois, all these questions and concerns had evaporated in the heat of that one objective.

Champlain stands waiting for them at the edge of the lake. The moment he saw the canoe, he knew it was Brulé. He breathed a deep sigh of relief, smiling, content that finally he had arrived. He knows Brulé will bring much needed clarity and direction. He always did.

The canoe slides into shallow water and Brulé steps out and wades to shore.

"You are early," shouts Champlain in greeting. "I did not think we would see you for several days yet. You must have got our message." Brulé approaches closer. But he does not respond immediately. As he embraces Champlain, his elation at having beaten the Iroquois gives way to anger. He feels suddenly incensed at the stupidity of their being out here at all, at the danger they are all exposed to. While still close to Champlain so no one else might hear, Brulé chastises him, "You are such a fool, coming now."

Champlain pulls back in surprise, "I have not seen you for over a year and you welcome me like that."

"Samuel, what in the name of hell are you doing here? And we did get that message, but off the tortured and mutilated bodies of those Algonquin. Whose stupid idea was that?"

At that, Champlain rolls his eyes and shakes his head, but before he can respond, Brulé suddenly notices Petashwa walking towards him. Wrapping his arm around the Algonquin's neck, he pulls his head towards him so that their foreheads touch. "It is good to see you, old friend."

"Good to see you, my brother."

Savignon leads the distraught LeCharon to shore. His robe, ripped and torn, his arms and legs lacerated and bleeding, the priest surveys his surroundings with a dull incomprehension, exhaustion and inner confusion.

"Samuel, you remember Father LeCharon," as Brulé introduces the priest. Champlain remembers the priest well, seated in his office a year ago, fresh from France. Bright, clear, alert. He looks at him now in dismay. Or at what is left of him. Du Barre, surprised to find the priest here, strides across the camp and now stands twenty feet away. He calls to him.

LeCharon looks up, searching for who has just spoken. Du Barre steps forward and calls his name again. LeCharon stares in wide-eyed confusion at the priest. "Woe to him, Brother, who preaches to others and himself is a castaway." He intones like some lost prophet. Du Barre studies him in horror as LeCharon hobbles towards him. He lifts him by the arm and leads him away from the others. Champlain embraces Savignon warmly, "Ah, my good friend, the Frenchman," he jokes. "And you Atsan. It is an honor to finally meet you. I have heard of you many times over the years,"

"You are a man now, Atsan," adds Petashwa, who has not seen Atsan in three or four years.

Champlain gestures towards de Valery, "The Count de Valery, Etienne Brulé." Brulé nods. "And The Marquis de Clemont." The Marquis remains a few feet away behind his elaborately set table, as if its presence might somehow ward off the untamed, wild power of this man who just stepped ashore. Again Brulé nods in greeting, but his expression is wary as he tries to understand why the two nobles are here.

"The wilderness suits you," he says to de Clemont, looking at his outfit. "I cannot imagine what blunder in court could have landed you here."

De Clemont flushes. He feels completely exposed, and so effortlessly. He glares at Brulé, and in his most condescending manner begins, "Well, really for someone…" But Brulé ignores him. He notices du Barre handing LeCharon a clean, neatly folded robe. Then he surveys the camp, assessing who's present, how many soldiers, their strength, the palisade, the number of canoes. He's immediately uneasy. Looking to Champlain, "What is going on here?"

"The whole trip is madness. The more so when you hear its purpose," answers Champlain. But the purpose now seems unimportant to Brulé and he pulls the conversation into focus. "Samuel, we have to break camp and go. We are surrounded by Iroquois. Or will be by morning. We must get out now."

"Iroquois!" Champlain exclaims. "Where? We have not seen any sign of them." He notices du Barre advancing quickly towards them. Brulé can feel the man's approach and turns.

"Father du Barre, I wish to introduce —" But the priest holds up a hand to stop Champlain. A fury bristles just behind the priest's mask of pious serenity, threatening to engulf it. Brulé's whole being leaps to attention before the priest. Not from fear, or at least bodily fear, but rather from the danger of a fanatical discipline and authority. The man exudes menace. Brulé feels it immediately. "I am not interested in pleasantries," the priest says. "A Jesuit priest has been murdered. Is that correct?" jutting his face towards Brulé.

"What?" cries Champlain.

"And what have you done to Father LeCharon? He is mad!" Du Barre doesn't speak so much as hiss and spit his words.

His ferocious intensity distracts Brulé, momentarily undermines his concentration and focus. The singular force of the priest's mind astonishes him. He quickly regroups, "You can worry about that later. Right now you have a bigger problem."

"There is no bigger problem than dealing with the murder of one of our Jesuit brothers by these savages. That we will deal with now. And we will begin with your part in it."

Champlain steps forward, impatient with the priest's misguided priorities. "Du Barre. Iroquois. You must understand. We are surrounded by Iroquois."

But Brulé perceives right away that Champlain's words have no effect on du Barre. Instead the priest's eyes narrow, he steps toward Brulé and pushes his face up close to his. "You think me a fool. I see through your game. You bring Father LeCharon here, what is left of him, Lord knows what horror you have put him through. You aim to scare us with this story of Iroquois, the dreaded Iroquois, so we run back to Québec, and you go home to your Wendat and this murderer goes free."

Brulé scrutinizes the fuming priest. He has lived for decades with only one reasonable response to Iroquois danger: complete attention and immediate action. The Iroquois created a visceral readiness. His plan for escape, everything he had been going over in his mind for two days, rests on everyone immediately understanding the danger. And acting. The priest's response takes him completely by surprise. Brulé points over to Savignon, Atsan and Tonda, who all immediately signal the need to act.

The priest flicks his hand in dismissal.

"Ask Charon. He saw — "

"I am not sure what Father LeCharon sees right now. Probably anything you want him to see. I have sent him to wash and change."

Brulé realizes any further exchange with this man wastes time. They have to stop talking and move forward with a concrete plan to escape. He looks to Champlain, but as he is about to speak, du Barre continues in a clipped fury, "I tell you what I propose. We go to the

Wendat as planned —"

"To the Wendat?" interrupts Brulé. In his mind, everyone needs to head across the lake in the exact opposite direction, and from there they might escape, or at least defend themselves.

"— as planned," continued du Barre, "We find this savage, we arrest him and hang him."

Brulé looks in disbelief at du Barre, thinking now he must be as mad as LeCharon. But it seems finally the danger posed by the Iroquois has at last registered with someone. Tales of their ferocious cruelty, tales perhaps exaggerated around the campfire at night, leap to de Valery's mind. "You say there are Iroquois?"

"They have guns," says Brulé.

"Guns!" cries Champlain. This thought terrifies him.

"And how are they getting guns?" du Barre asks as if to a lying child, another ploy Brulé has perhaps invented to frighten them.

"The English do not seem to care for the Iroquois soul the way you Jesuits care for the Wendat," answers Brulé.

At this moment, laughter erupts from the other side of camp. Brulé knows this sound only too well from Québec. He looks over at four Algonquin sitting on the far side of camp. As he turns back to du Barre, the priest continues, "You know we will consider trading guns with any savage willing to convert and prove their fidelity to Christ."

"We need guns now," replies Brulé.

"Then perhaps this will fuel their faith in Christ," adds the priest. Brulé, has forced himself to resist the constant undertow of the priest's intensity pulling the focus away from what must be done. But this final comment breaks the spell. He says to Champlain "You have to do something. You have to save yourselves."

For the last few weeks, ever since du Barre had belittled and undermined his leadership, Champlain has busied himself with his maps and journals. But now, recognizing du Barre's complete failure to grasp their danger, his natural instinct to command reasserts itself. "Du Barre, we must break camp. Now. You have —"

The priest ignores Champlain and thrusts back directly at Brulé, "I have a mandate. From Cardinal Richelieu personally. Nothing will interfere with that. Not you. Or your Iroquois scare."

"You have a mandate to do what?"

Brulé had put all his questions about Champlain's presence out here to the back of his mind but that one word — mandate — brings his queries back with a force. What was this mandate that so gripped this priest's mind that it blocked common sense?

"Why are you out here?"

"To colonize this land for the glory of France and the glory of God," proclaims the priest, spitting out each word as if to rub it in his face.

"I've seen what the French do in the name of God," counters Brulé. "But this is no place for a colony."

And as the words leave his mouth suddenly the full impact of the man's statement hits him. "The Wendat. You want to colonize the Land of the Wendat." Brulé had succeeded in keeping the French out for over two decades and now an expedition wasn't just visiting the Land of the Wendat, they wanted to occupy it. He yells as he jabs a finger hard against du Barre's chest, "They live there damn it."

Du Barre steps back, shocked and affronted by Brulé's aggressive gesture. No one, ever, treats him like that. "They have lived there forever and what have they got to show for it? Some bark huts. We want to build something permanent. Roads, Towns."

"On Wendat land?"

"This is French land. Governed by French law. Our authority comes from God. And from the Crown. These savages need the yoke of Christ."

With these last words, something breaks in Brulé. A fraction of a second later his tomahawk smashes once, twice, three times on the crystal and china set on the nobles' table beside him. Shards, chips and splinters of glass and porcelain fly and bounce around him as the two nobles gape in disbelief at the destruction.

But those few physical blows, release his anger and Brulé's head is clear. He turns to du Barre, "You are naked here. God and your laws can do nothing. You have no idea the hell that is about to come down on you."

Du Barre again steps back before Brulé's fury. Clearly, he knows that Brulé would have preferred those blows had come down on his head. But he rallies himself, steels his right of authority. He speaks with a sense of forced, aloof disdain, "I am sure you understand hell, Brulé. Or, if you do not, you will. This is a Catholic colony. And I want you out of it."

Brulé turns to Champlain, "You need to do something Samuel or you will all die."

"We will not be frightened by you into returning to Québec. Cardinal Richelieu himself has commanded me and we will continue. We will go to the Land of the Wendat and claim it for France. We will find the one responsible for the murder of Father Marquette, and we will arrest him."

Brulé realizes that if they are to succeed with this escape, he must ignore this man and team with Champlain. But the vast affront and incomprehension of the priest pulls him back in.

"Arrest him? Just walk into their village and take him. What are you thinking? You say you want to live there and you start with that."

"These savages must understand the meaning of French law and justice."

"They will cut you to pieces."

"Then guns for the Wendat would hardly be timely would they? I will see this savage is tried and hung."

Brulé, tomahawk still in hand, now slams it down on the noble's table itself, splitting it in two. With this one final blow, the last vestige of the nobles' civilized property has been destroyed, lying now splintered and useless at their feet.

Brulé is furious that he has let this priest get to him again. Behind du Barre, he sees LeCharon stepping into the water just beyond the gap at the end of the palisade. Near the priest, two soldiers talk. One leans against the edge of the palisade, the other nestles himself in the fork of a tree to have a view over the palisade wall into the forest. Another burst of laughter escapes from the four Algonquin on the other side of camp. A drunken laughter. And not far from them, six French men lounge against the palisade wall.

"Who are they?" Brulé asks.

"The company's new men," answers du Barre. "Those that will replace you."

But Brulé is already striding towards them. His frustration and fury with the priest now overflow at the sight unfolding before him. He hated nothing more than seeing the French give alcohol to the Wendat when they came to Québec. He hates what it did to them. And what it has done to the Algonquin.

As Brulé approaches closer, one of the aides rises to welcome him, oblivious of what is about to be unleashed. Brulé grabs the man by the throat, lifting him off the ground and pins him against a tree. Two aides rush to help. Lightening fast, Brulé's tomahawk swings up, clipping one man on the jaw, and he sprawls back onto the ground. The second attacker stops, Brulé's tomahawk poised above his head.

"Sit down."

The attacker backs away and sits. Brulé swings the butt of his tomahawk head into the groin of the man he holds by the neck. The man howls in agony, his eyes bulge, he can't breath. Brulé pulls the tomahawk back and turns it over. "This time I cut them off. Where is it?"

He tightens his grip on the man's neck, his face by now almost purple, "One, two…"

The man gestures madly with one hand. Brulé turns to the aide nearest him. "Get it." The man hesitates and Brulé again lifts his tomahawk up to strike. The man in Brulé's grip wails and the aid scurries to a nearby pack. "Open it." He unties the straps and tips it on its side. Blankets, two rolls of canvas and then four one-gallon wooden casks roll onto the ground.

"Is there more?" Brulé clenches his throat tighter. He shakes his head and Brulé releases him. He drops to his knees gagging and sucking for air. Brulé pulls out his second tomahawk and in four swift blows, a tomahawk in each hand, he splits the casks. Rum pours out. He rolls each cask with his foot, making sure they are empty. Then he walks back to the aides. He drops down to one knee so his eyes are level with theirs.

"If I catch you bringing alcohol to the Wendat I will gut you like a fish." They eye him like deer before a wolf. He stares hard at each of them in turn, then gets up. "All this for some Goddamn hats in Paris."

Brulé feels better, energized from actually doing something, as he walks back to Champlain. He is convinced that despite all the priest's outrageous interruptions, they might still get everyone away across the lake in time.

As Brulé passes, the priest tries to assure him that he'd been promised there would be no trade in alcohol. But Brulé ignores him. He turns instead to Champlain, "Samuel, we came to warn you. We need guns. The Wendat are finished without them. The fur trade is finished. Québec is finished. I am leaving now for Québec. Join me and I think we can still make it to safety. If you do not, none of you will make it alive. It is your decision."

Witnessing Brulé's new resolve, Champlain's own sense of command returns, "Good. We break camp."

Stunned at this sudden shift in power, du Barre protests, "What? What are you saying? No! Absolutely not." De Clement suddenly realizes this is his chance; this is the moment to put his own plan into action. "Yes, we will break camp. Here," he beckons to his three French soldiers. As they hustle over, he announces, "We are going. And these men will take us."

Champlain's revived claim on authority enrages du Barre. But if he is also confounded and angered by de Clemont he doesn't show it. He looks now at the Marquis, turns his imperious attention on him and holds it there. De Clemont's mind quickly clouds and falters in the face of the priest's glare. The priest looks at the three soldiers. "He will desert you when you get back to France. He will not protect you because he will not even be able to protect himself. Come back to me now and I may be lenient. Otherwise all three of you are dead men. I guarantee it in the name of the King." With this threat, du Barre reassumes his authority, at least over the soldiers who as yet have no sense of the severity of Iroquois threat. He gestures and two more soldiers scurry over.

"Brulé, you are under arrest. You are coming with us." Du Barre motions to the five soldiers now beside him. They level their muskets at Brulé, who looks at the musket barrels pointed at him and then up at the priest.

"For what?"

"I do not really need a reason. Accomplice to murder will do. I am putting you in irons."

At these words, Champlain explodes. He has had it with du Barre. He yells in frustration at the priest until two soldiers swing their barrels towards him. Du Barrre continues to Brulé, "After our trip to the Wendat, you are going back to France. This shameless black existence of yours is over. I have had enough of your Iroquois ruse."

"For God's sake du Barre, you are mad!" says Champlain seething, keenly aware the momentum for escape is slipping away.

"I see exactly what he is trying to do. Scaring us off. He does not fool me."

Two of the soldiers on sentry duty watch the growing confrontation on the other side of camp. They are charged with guarding their end of the palisade and right now with watching over the disoriented LeCharon as he washes in the lake next to the palisade gate. One should be standing at the gate scanning the length of the wall; the other, perched in the fork of a tree, should be surveying the forest over the palisade wall. But both are distracted, drawn into the drama unfolding not thirty feet away.

As the soldiers level their muskets at Brulé, one of the sentries says, "That man knows how to get himself in a fix." They turn back now as LeCharon straightens his new robe and steps out from behind the bushes in the shallow water onto shore not ten feet away. At that instant, an arrow shoots through the neck of the sentry in the tree.

Brulé whirls at the sudden sound, intuiting danger. He bolts before the sentry's gun even hits the ground. Smashing the soldiers' gun barrels aside, he races across the camp. As he runs, he sees two Iroquois grab LeCharon still just outside the palisade and disappear. The other sentry, shocked momentarily, now swings his musket and aims at the Iroquois dragging away LeCharon. But two other Iroquois have worked their way silently along the outside of the palisade. They knock the sentry down and begin dragging him into the woods.

Blind to the scene unfolding behind him, du Barre assumes Brulé is trying to escape. "Stop him," he yells. The soldiers shoulder their muskets and take aim. But Tonda and Atsan lunge forward smashing the barrels and the shots go wild.

Brulé grabs the sentry's musket lying below the tree, dives for the edge of the palisade on his belly and raises the gun. The two Iroquois with LeCharon disappear into the forest and are gone. The other two drag the soldier. He aims and fires just as one of the Iroquois leans forward to get a better grasp of the soldier's arm. The bullet hits the Iroquois in the back and he sprawls forward into the others. But in an instant, they too disappear into the forest and are gone.

Another sentry further down the palisade, whose shot had gone wide through the trees, yells, "You hit him."

"Damn," curses Brulé. He hadn't been aiming at the Iroquois. "Poor wretch," he mutters, knowing what awaits the captured soldier.

He looks up, aware of a strange, gurgling sound. The sentry's body hangs above him, his leg wedged in the fork of the tree. The arrow passed through his throat, and blood from the wound pours over his face and down the trunk. Brulé takes his knife and digs into the man's neck and twists. The soldier's entire body convulses and then goes limp.

The soldiers, after firing wildly, had chased after Brulé to stop his supposed escape. They stand now, stunned at what they have just witnessed. Du Barre follows behind, his pace betraying his alarm.

"What is going on? What has happened?" asks du Barre, his aloof assurance slightly less intact. "Where is Jean-Philippe? Damn it, what happened? Where is he?" Finally, Brulé realizes, the danger and reality of their situation are beginning to dawn on this man.

"Your Iroquois ruse just took him."

"What do you mean just took him? Where? We have to get him back."

"Go ask them," says Brulé, gesturing towards the forest.

Now, he thinks, now, even du Barre will see what they must do. And perhaps this capture will give them some advantage. He knows these new prisoners will engross the Iroquois. For hours. This could give them the time they need to get away across the lake. Just as he is about to open his mouth to corral everyone to that end, du Barre says, "We must get him back. How do we get him back?" He clutches Brulé's arm, but Brulé's thoughts are now totally focused on their path of escape.

"It will be dark in an hour. We leave everything here but canoes and muskets and hope we can find a place to defend ourselves on the Smoke River. They will know now that we will try to escape. Our hope of slipping away after dark, unnoticed, is gone. But they will be slow in their elm-bark canoes and we—"

"No, no, no. How do we save Jean-Philippe?"

Brulé can't believe it; still the priest persists. "You mean from the Iroquois?"

Du Barre nods at him, a desperate look gripping his face.

"Forget him. Do you hear me? Forget him. They may save him for ransom. He is worth more alive than dead. You need to think of everyone else here. We need to save them. Now."

"Will they hurt him?" the priest pleads.

"I hate to think what they will do to him. But they may not kill him."

"What —?"

"You do not want to know," cautions Brulé.

"I convinced him to come here. I cannot leave him," cries du Barre. Then in almost a whisper, "He is my brother."

But Brulé's attention is on the task at hand. He ignores the priest's comment, assuming he means all Jesuits are his brothers. "This in fact may give us a chance. The Iroquois will be busy with them all night. We can —"

"No, no, no...you do not understand. My brother. My younger brother."

The words stop Brulé. He lets out a long sigh as the pieces fit, "LeCharon du Barre. Du Barre better suits your ambitions in court. LeCharon befits the humble priest."

"Please," pleads du Barre. He implores Champlain, the soldiers, the nobles, but he has made no allies, and they avert their gaze. Suddenly, the priest's pious, arrogant bearing has transformed into desperate pleading.

He appeals to Brulé, his eyes betraying his fear, "Help me. I cannot leave him," he whispers.

As Brulé witnesses this once-powerful, willful priest wilt before him, out of nowhere, he has an idea. A crazy, half-formed, mad idea. He looks at Tonda, Atsan and Savignon, at Champlain and Petashwa and then out across the wide, free expanse of the lake in the last light of evening. The wheels turn, new pieces jump into place, the initial madness of it begins to evolve into a rash scheme. The faint but fantastic possibility slowly becomes tangible and concrete in his mind.

Except for the sentries alert now at their posts around the palisade, everyone stands silent around Brulé and du Barre, the camp suspended in a quiet vacuum of thought as this tumbling of cogs and gears drops into place in Brulé's mind. As the last piece locks into place, he closes his eyes and feels the whole structure clear and anchored within him. He holds it there until he owns it, then opens his eyes and stares straight at du Barre.

"I will rescue Charon."

"Thank you. We must——" begins the priest.

"This is what I want in return."

The priest hadn't anticipated this response; he looks at Brulé suspiciously.

"I stay with the Wendat. The trade arrangement remains the same."

Du Barre's manner already begins to shift. He has embedded himself, lodged himself, within the authority of the Crown, a Divine authority. He has realized his identity through that authority. No one dictates to the Crown. "I cannot do that. We have a company of investors now. A new colony."

But Brulé ignores him and continues, "You drop these charges of murder."

Revolt and anger surge through the priest's mind. He will not relinquish his need for justice and order, and he most certainly will not relinquish the need for revenge. "He murdered a Jesuit. I cannot ignore that."

"Is he more important than your brother?"

Du Barre seethes, his breath a rasping snarl. He hates Brulé and had relished the moment he would crush him. Now instead, this uncouth savage dominates him and he loathes it. Looking out across the lake, he ferrets desperately for some escape from his futility and the fury eating at him. But he sees nothing. Jean-Philippe, a younger brother, who looked up to him, whom he protected when they were young, who followed his advice, whom he guided, and cared for and steered to the priesthood and even encouraged to come here, that most honorable role of missionary, which — and this now sears du Barre to his core — he had thought, in the grip of his own clawing ambition, might serve him well in court.

"And I want two hundred muskets."

"Two hundred!" The priest chokes in his vexation.

"I have a people to protect, not just a village."

With each demand du Barre's rebellion against his powerlessness erupts further; he rages at his own impotence.

"The Iroquois know some of you are worth money, a lot more than furs. That is why they are here and not attacking the Wendat. They will wipe out this party and take you, and Samuel and those two, torture you, and sell your breathing carcasses to the English. Richelieu will have to bargain and pay for your release and you will return to France, broken, disgraced and disfigured. Finished. Richelieu will abandon New France. Which all suits me fine. All if I do nothing. But I need guns."

"Torture?" De Clemont grasps de Valery's sleeve in panic.

De Valery, suddenly alert to what could unfold, asks, "Why are they not attacking us now?"

"They need light to take hostages," replies Brulé. "They have a couple of French to torture now. Then they will attack in the morning. They do not think you can get away."

Du Barre feels everyone's eyes on him. He had orchestrated his authority carefully with those on the expedition. He created a cult of it, elevated himself and buried all intimacies and allies. Now, as he looks to Champlain, the nobles and his soldiers, he sees he is completely alone.

Then de Clemont yells, "God damn it, du Barre, get us out of here!" and that one comment severs whatever vestiges of control the priest still held. Everyone clamours at once — soldiers, aides, Champlain, the nobles. His tightly defined fabric of authority unravels, its dynamic swiftly shifting. His ambition, his imperious certainty, his divine authority break and dissolve before him. The reality of what lies ahead he now faces for the first time.

"I cannot leave him. I cannot," he says amid the noise of the company's shifting loyalties and search for direction. Suddenly, he bellows, a long howl of frustration and fury, "This dumb brute of a Godless land!" The entire company falls silent, staring as this receptacle and edifice of the crown, crushed and chastened, slumps in defeat.

Brulé turns to Champlain, the reins of leadership firm in his hands. He realizes how their plan can unfold, every past delay, in fact, now feeding into their success. It is possible. But far from certain.

"Samuel, write a statement with my three points, for the same trade arrangement, for the case against the Wendat who killed Marquette and for the guns. I want both of you and du Barre to sign it. Petashwa, my friend, I need you to take the letter to Québec. Now. Leave now, with two Algonquin. You can be on the Smoke River and out of danger before anything happens here with the Iroquois."

"But Etienne," says Champlain, "we do not have two hundred muskets in Québec."

Brulé grasps the two satchels of gold coins from Atsan who has just retrieved them from their canoe. "We will get forty now and you can order the rest to come with the ships next spring from France." He passes the two bags to Petashwa, "It is the life of the Wendat you hold in your hands, my brother."

Petashwa takes the gold, "You have my word, Etienne."

Du Barre gazes on the scene, numb and defeated, his influence stripped and spent. He thinks about the court, knowing what is going on at this very moment here in camp sounds the death knell of his career. There will be nothing but mockery from Richelieu for this.

"The Iroquois will leave a group to guard their canoes," Brulé explains to Champlain. "The others will be here, waiting to attack at daybreak. At first light, I will attack the Iroquois camp with Atsan, Savignon and Tonda. You must be ready at that moment to escape. When the Iroquois hear our attack, those who are here will race back to protect their canoes. Otherwise they will be stranded. In their mind, you have no escape. They think they have you. If Charon is alive and we escape, we will catch up to you."

It sounds good. Almost reasonable. But the plan is desperate, mad, cobbled together in crisis. Yet he has set it in motion and would not change it now. He motions to Atsan, Savignon and Tonda. Moving away from the rest of the company, they gather in a circle facing one another.

Brulé outlines what must unfold step by step. Tonda's eyes grow bright, his broad muscular body beginning to twitch in anticipation — fearless, impatient even for the fight ahead. Live or die, this is what Tonda feels he is made for. This plan of Brulé's fills him with a vast relief. Atsan feels himself swell into it. Tonda begins to chant. A war chant. He leads and the other three join in. He takes his knife and makes a short deep cut in his forearm. A thick line of blood flows down his arm into his hand. The others do the same. They join hands, their blood mingling, and then each draws three lines of blood on their upper arm and then on the person next to them. "One blood, one life," declares Tonda, concluding the ceremony, but not the pledge or the power of what they have just done. They will live or die together in this. Brulé's eyes meet Atsan's. They gleam in anticipation.

As they conclude their vow and bond, Champlain calls to Savignon. In his hands, he holds a beautiful, new, brocade and velvet frock coat, masterfully crafted, a deep, rich blue with green trim. "I will keep it for you and give it to you tomorrow," he says. But Savignon shakes his head and takes it from him. The two nobles marvel at how fresh and clean it is, reminding them of home and civilization.

Savignon holds it up. Then he pulls out his knife and cuts into the sleeves at the shoulder and rips them both off, so it is sleeveless like his old one. The two nobles stare in disbelief at the destruction, reminding them yet again of how fragile civilization seems out here. Savignon takes off the old coat, puts on the new one and reties his belt over it. He looks at it grimly, knowing he will take this new prize to battle.

De Valery puts his hand on Savignon's arm, "I will tell her, Savignon, how brave you looked going to fight in your new coat." His words surprise him for they acknowledge clearly and without doubt the gravity and danger of what these four men are about to attempt on their behalf. Savignon looks him in the eye, but de Valery has never before seen a look like that.

An hour later, Brulé walks down to the shore with Champlain. "Petashwa will be across the lake by now and safely away." Atsan, Savignon and Tonda are already in the canoe. He knows he must turn to say goodbye to Champlain, but hesitates, aware he avoids the man. He doesn't want any emotion, any cracks of sympathy or sorrow invading the grim resolve he now feels and must sustain. Brulé gives him a quick hug and sees the tears in Champlain's eyes. "I will see you in the morning, Samuel," he assures him as he gets in the canoe. They push off and disappear into the dark.

Du Barre watches as their canoe slips into the night. A loon calls out from across the lake. The wild, crazy cry of the loon. And then almost in answer, in the far distance, a scream, the wild, terrible scream of a man. Du Barre's face turns the picture of terror.


They paddle well out from shore in the dark, the light of the moon diffuse behind high clouds. The French camp lies four hundred yards behind them now. With each stroke of their paddles they pull, then rotated to slide them forward through the water, then pull again. The blade never leaves the water for fear the moving, wet blade might catch some reflection and alert a watchful Iroquois. Their paddles make no sound. But in truth the Iroquois are engaged. Their bodies, covered in sweat and the grease of war paint, gleam as they dance around their huge bonfire. They drum and scream and wail.

Brulé puts down his paddle and pulls out a small, brass telescope. He focuses on the camp, the number of Iroquois, the canoes, the layout. A wall of rock surrounds and protects the campsite. He has in fact camped here himself in the past. A number of Iroquois file out through a narrow gap in the rock wall. They head to the French camp in preparation to attack in the morning. He swings the telescope back to the camp and sees the French soldier. He's tied to a tree behind the fire, his face and chest bloody and burnt. An Iroquois raises a red-hot knife to his face. He sees the whites of the soldier's eyes, wild with pain and fear, when the knife touches his face in a cloud of smoke. They can hear his scream above the din of the Iroquois.

Totiri, the Iroquois war chief, brings a shimmering hot tomahawk up close to Brulé's face. He twists violently away from both the telescope and his own searing memory. He's immediately covered in sweat and breaths heavily. Tonda puts his hand on his shoulder to steady him. He breathes long and deep, his eyes closed, collecting himself. Finally he nods and picks up his paddle. "I do not see Charon. He is not the one on the stake."

They glide past the Iroquois camp and continue towards the huge, dark outcrop of granite they'd seen from across the lake earlier that afternoon. It rises straight out of the water. The sounds of drumming and the screaming and the light from the fire continue as they paddle along the sheer face of rock. But then, turning a sharp corner, they are out of sight of the camp. The sounds immediately seem far away.

Examining the wall rising a hundred and fifty feet above them, they locate a small ledge at water level they can step on to. Brulé lands, swings a musket over each shoulder and ties them around his waist with a rope secure for the climb. He stuffs two pistols and his moccasins into his belt and secures them tightly. He also ties one end of a length of rope to his belt. He looks up at the sheer face and then, finding a foothold, he hoists himself up. He searches for a handhold above him and finds another foothold and moves a step higher. Savignon and Atsan each tie two muskets secure for the climb and start up, following Brulé.

Last, Tonda steps onto the ledge. He kneels and levers a large rock, sliding it as slowly as he can into the canoe so it doesn't make noise. It punctures the soft bark and the canoe fills with water. It begins to sink, slowly disappearing into the dark depths of the lake, leaving no trace of their presence. Then Tonda heads up after the others.

Pressed against the face of the rock wall, Brulé stops his climb and gazes down eighty feet to the black shimmering water and the others climbing below him. His route up the wall has good footholds, but is hard to read in the dark. He climbs further until he finds himself below an overhang. Not large, but as he tries to get his hand out over the top of it, he almost loses his grip on the wall. A long, vertical seam of rock obstructs his moving to the left. He tries moving to the right to see if he can find a gap in the overhang. But each time he finds a foothold to move right, the overhang blocks his climb. He keeps scraping his way over until he finds a wide, vertical cleft in the rock wall too wide to cross. He is stuck and it is too dark to try and go back down.

He calls softly to the others below to search for another route up. Tonda, the lowest down, can easily get on the other side of the vertical crack that has blocked Brulé. It opens up a completely different route. Brulé unties the rope from his waist and drops it to Savignon who drops it to Tonda, who starts up the new route. He comes to a smooth, sheer pitch. He presses himself to the wall and claws his way with his toes and fingernails. At one point his toes slip but his fingers claw the rock for anything and he holds on, pressing his knees and forearms tight in against the rock. He scrapes his way up the smooth section, finds a fissure, pushes his hands and feet into it and rests. It runs straight up and he can jam his hands and feet into it to find good purchase now on this new course up to a small ledge where he can stand. He is still twenty feet below Brulé but can see the overhang and the wide, gaping vertical cut that obstructs him. From the ledge where he now stands, Tonda sees the climb ahead is less steep and thirty feet above him leads to grasses and then small shrubs and finally to trees at the top.

He unties the rope at his waist, jams it deep into a wedge of rock and wraps it tight. He throws one end to Savignon who ties it to his waist and jumps out, swinging over the vertical fissure, landing on the smooth face of granite and pulling himself hand over hand quickly making his way up to Tonda. Atsan has climbed up almost level to Tonda who tosses the other end of the rope across to him. He swings over and clambers up to the ledge as well.

As the others move up to the ledge with Tonda, Brulé tries to work back the way he came, but he can find no footholds below that will support him. He's stuck where he is.

Tonda frees the rope from the rock. He motions to Atsan and Savignon to start climbing further up the slope to give him more room to throw. He coils the rope and flings it high towards Brulé. It hangs uncoiling in space but well below him and then falls down across the rock face. He coils it again, tighter and heaves the rope in a long arc, closer but still below Brulé. He coils the rope again but it cannot be thrown high enough and far enough for Brulé to catch it. Although the climbing is easier above the ledge from where he stands, up there Tonda sees no place to secure the rope; if Brulé's weight were to pull on it both he and Brulé would be dragged off the rock face.

But Brulé has watched the arc of the rope carefully and calls over to Tonda to throw again. Tonda once more coils it and with a lunging swing throws as far and high as he can. It arches up, unfurling in a ghostly tangle in the pale moonlight as it rises. At that instant Brulé leaps off the rock wall into space. The line finishes its climb and hangs for a moment as he swings his right hand into the arabesque of curling rope. But the piece he lunges at is falling faster than he anticipated and his hand passes wide. He swings again with his left hand grasping at another section. Both he and the line are dropping fast. He feels the cord in his hand, slipping, passing through his fingers. He is free-falling now and must somehow ensnare himself in the rope to break his fall. He throws his arm into a quickly closing loop while twisting his body into another tightening noose beside him. The loose tangle and the arc of Brulé's fall ends in a wrenching jolt just as he smashes hard into the rock. The impact sends a stabbing pain through his left shoulder as the line gashes deep into his arms and across his chest. He hangs limp, but firmly caught.

Tonda has the other end secure and begins to haul him upwards. Brulé's arms are entwined in the rope but with his feet he manages to ascend the rock wall until he is beside Tonda. Atsan and Savignon, seeing Brulé safe below, continue to climb. The rock soon gives way to a steep slope of grasses and bushes. They clamber up and into the trees at the top. Tonda and Brulé soon join them.

They quickly scout for Iroquois sentries. But no one seems to be up here, never imagining anyone attempting to climb the rock face or attack their camp. Through the trees, the land falls away again in front of them in a steep, forested drop. They see the Iroquois fire far below and again hear the drumming, singing, and the screams of terror and pain.

They work their way down the forested slope. At the bottom Brulé slips through the last of the trees and crawls on his belly into the tall grasses on the edge of the clearing, the others moving silently beside him. To their right, fifteen canoes, neatly arrayed, line the shore. The steep, forested slope they have just descended becomes a steep rock wall along the back of the clearing. The same wall wraps around to the far side of the clearing creating a semi-circle of rock along the shore. A vertical crack, wide enough for a man to pass through, splits the enclosure on the far side. This was the gap Brulé saw through his telescope earlier. The one he had seen the Iroquois using to leave the clearing. He knows, from having camped here himself, that that sliver of space forms a long cleft in the rock that opens out eventually near the point of land of Champlain's camp.

In the middle of the clearing, the fire, and behind the fire, tied to a tree, the French soldier slumps unconscious. An Iroquois slaps the soldier trying to revive him.

Brulé sees LeCharon. He lies curled up, his back to them. He counts sixteen Iroquois dancing around the fire. Based on the number of canoes, he estimates that thirty or more must be surrounding the French camp waiting for daybreak. He notices a dozen muskets leaning near the gap in the wall.

Brulé takes his two muskets, checks their charge. He checks the charge in his two pistols, and replaces them in his belt. He lays both his tomahawks in front of him and places both muskets carefully beside him. He checks that the others have one musket aimed and ready to fire and the second at the ready, then he takes a powder horn from his belt. A wick hangs from one of the capped ends. He cups his hands around the flint as he strikes it into the wick. The spark catches the powder in the wick and it starts to burn. He turns, holding the powder horn, watching the wick burn down, waiting, and then throws it high into the air above the clearing. It arcs up and then explodes in a startling flash of light and smoke.

The Iroquois stop, stunned. Four muskets fire and four Iroquois drop. But it takes only a moment for them to recover. One Iroquois points to the cloud of smoke at the edge of the clearing. Knowing the guns can only fire once, they charge, howling as one.

Brulé drops the first musket, picks up the second and aims. He fires and hears the volley of three others. Three more Iroquois drop. Brulé scrambles to his feet, hands on his tomahawks, flying into the Iroquois just as they reach him. He parries the blow of a club with his left axe, stepping right to miss the brunt of the blow as a warrior plows into him. Swinging with his right axe, he cuts deep into the man's neck. He leaps forward into a second Iroquois just as the warrior's axe whistles by his head. The Iroquois's momentum knocks Brulé backwards off his feet. The Iroquois raises his knife to strike as they both go down. But before they hit the ground, Brulé has a pistol at the man's head and fires.

He pushes free and jumps to his feet, turning towards Atsan. His son blocks a blow, and then a second against an Iroquois. Brulé fires the second pistol at the warrior and he drops. Tonda, knowing neither Savignon nor Atsan are tested in battle, cuts straight across the Iroquois' path swinging and breaking the fury of their attack.

But Brulé hasn't moved. After firing the second pistol he feels something on the far side of the clearing. He turns and watches Totiri, the Iroquois war chief, emerge through the gap in the rock wall.

Totiri, the black and red paint on his face lit by the fire, surveys the fight. He sees Brulé and strides across the clearing, pulling out both his tomahawks. He attacks, raining down a flurry of blows on Brulé, who parries and blocks them and jumps back out of the way. They circle one another. Each looks for the moment to strike, for a tiny crack in the other's mental armor. A lightening blow, and another. The blows of the war chief come down in a blur; they pour down. Brulé blocks, parries, dodges. He's forced back. His left shoulder, where he smashed into the rock wall on his climb, now shrieks in pain as he is forced to deflect each blow from the war chief's powerful right arm. All of Brulé's attention goes to defending himself. He steps back again and again. He can feel the edge of the clearing closer and closer behind him, trapping him.

Then Savignon slashes into the fight. Totiri senses him coming and parries the blow. Both Brulé and Savingon attack, swinging hard and fast. Yet Totiri blocks them, twisting and dodging. Even with the two of them they can't get a blow to land. The war chief is magnificent. Forced back, with four tomahawks slashing at him, he blocks and counters the blows, senses the dead lying on the ground behind him, stepping over them. He misses nothing.

Isolated by the fire, LeCharon finally stirs. He stares at his smashed, bloody hands, but then suddenly notices the dead body beside him. An Iroquois. He looks up terrified, trying to understand what is happening. He sees Brulé and Savignon raining blows down on Totiri, forcing him back tep by step by step, closer and closer to Le Charon. He is directly in their path. Then he sees it, on the ground in front of him, the dead Iroquois's knife.

Brulé and Savingon gain on Totiri, but a lightening flick of a backstroke across Savignon's jaw and he staggers back out of the fight and onto his knees.. Once again, Brulé is on his own. He knows he cannot fight Totiri alone for long. He pours down blows on the war chief, clearly his last attack. Totiri steps back once, twice, three times, until he stands almost beside LeCharon. Then the tide turns. Totiri gains the upper hand and starts hammering heavy blows in a fury. His one desire — to finish Brulé, now.

Two ruined, bloody hands hold a knife. LeCharon, crawling to his knees, falls forward, holding the knife tight against his chest and sinks it with one desperate stroke into the calf of the war chief beside him. The pain shoots through LeCharon's broken hands but the knife cuts deep just at the moment the war chief shifts his weight to that leg.

Totiri grimaces, stumbles and at that instant Brulé blocks a blow and swings his axe into Totiri's arm cutting the muscle to the bone. He swings with his other axe, but Totiri blocks it and begins another furious onslaught with only his left arm. Stunned by the ferocity of the attack Brulé steps back once, twice, but after a dozen blows the war chief slows, his right arm hanging useless. The Iroquois swings with another defiant blow. Brulé deflects it, then steps around and drives his right tomahawk deep into Totiri's skull. He drops to his knees. As Brulé yanks the axe loose, Totiri slumps over, dead.

At that moment, he hears the distant shouts of the Iroquois. He knew they would return to protect their canoes. The sound ricochets down the long gorge and out the narrow gap in the rock wall of the clearing.

Savignon kneels several feet away. Blood pours out of the cut on his jaw and runs in a red stream down the rich blue of his new coat as he gets to his feet.

"Get Charon in a canoe," Brulé says as he runs past him to Atsan. His son also staggers to his feet, blood on his face and chest, an Iroquois lying dead beside him. Brulé runs his hands over his cuts but Atsan pulls back.

"I'm not hurt. Tonda saved me twice. He …" but he trails off, both of them now looking at the Wendat war chief, on his knees, covered in blood. Four dead Iroquois lie sprawled around him.

"Help Savingon," says Brulé and he steps over to Tonda, only just conscious, dying. Brulé runs his fingers through a deep cut in Tonda's neck and wipes the Wendat blood on his own arms. Then he takes more blood and wipes it on his lips.

"I take your blood to battle, my brother." Then, with a tomahawk in each hand, he runs to the canoes. With both axes flying he smashes holes in the fragile elm bark. Chips fly as he works his way down the line of canoes.

Savignon readies a sleek, birch bark canoe, almost certainly the one taken from Petashwa's assistant. LeCharon stumbles, broken and shattered, as Atsan drags him to the lake.

Again the cries of the Iroquois catch their attention, echoing down the rock walls through the gap. Closer now.

The first light of morning glows a pale yellow on the horizon. Brulé can see the canoes of Champlain's party escaping across the lake.

They help LeCharon into the canoe. The priest looks up at Brulé. Their eyes lock for one brief second in a connection that somehow transcends the havoc and desperation around them. "Thou shalt be with me in Paradise," the priest whispers. The screams of the advancing Iroquois break the moment.

Yet, now for the second time, the priest reveals the path Brulé must take. He must stay. They've smashed the canoes so that the Iroquois cannot chase Champlain's party. Now they have no canoes to return home. But thirty or more Iroquois with guns, furious and vengeful, would go by foot to the Wendat for canoes and kill and destroy whomever and whatever they could.

"Savignon, look at that gap in the rock. We could defend that. Both of us. We can destroy them here. Finish them. Whoever is left will not attack the Wendat."

Savignon looks across the lake at Champlain escaping and then down at the smashed canoes.

"They will attack the Wendat on foot, Savignon. We can stop them here. Now."

Atsan, about to get in the canoe behind LeCharon, stops. "I am staying with you."

"No, Atsan. Take him. Go." He almost screams the order at his son. He knows how harsh it sounds, but he cannot begin to say what he really feels might lie ahead, or speak of his feelings for his son now standing before him.

"But —"

"You must get Charon to Champlain. That is our deal for the guns.

That depends on you now. You must do that, Atsan. Go. "

Standing in the shallow water by the canoe, Atsan walks back to Brulé and throws his arms around him. Brulé holds him, breathes him in and kisses the top of his head. "That dog Totiri is dead. His village weak. When you get home, attack his village, take your mother and her children and bring them home to the Wendat."

Brulé pushes his son toward the canoe, steadies it as he climbs in and then shoves the canoe out into the lake. Atsan takes his paddle and digs in for two strokes. He looks back one last time, tears welling up in his eyes, then quickly turns and paddles hard and determined after Champlain. LeCharon fumbles with a paddle in his broken hands, drops it and then slumps back, staring listlessly out across the lake.

The screams now seem closer, louder, echoing down the long, rock gorge. Brulé picks up one end of a smashed canoe and drags it toward the rock wall. Savignon drags a second. They wedge them, one on top of the other, between two trees and the gap in the rock face. They now have a five-foot barrier blocking the only possible entry back into the clearing.

They run and collect the dozen muskets leaning against the wall and gather the eight others they had brought. Savignon checks and loads furiously as Brulé takes two burning sticks from the fire and jams them into two canoes, setting the dry bark alight. He rushes back to help Savignon load. The cries seem almost on top of them now. But looking down the length of the rock-walled gorge, Brulé still cannot yet see any Iroquois.

"We can do real damage here Savignon. Real damage…for awhile."

Once into the steep-walled gorge, the Iroquois will have only one defense, straight into their musket fire. They will know this. It will begin and end here, now, decided in one furious onslaught. He's propelled now, keen and alive, he sees, to the very human destruction he so abhorred, to the destruction he had sworn himself against.

Fire spreads rapidly along the line of dry bark canoes. The early dawn light illuminates the gorge.

"I needed you," Brulé says to Savignon, feeling a pang of remorse for pulling his companion into this mad scheme.

"I needed it too, Etienne," says Savignon. "To be a warrior for my people. To have a song sung of this. Although no one may know of it."

"They'll know, Savignon."

They load muskets, leaning them side-by-side, immediately at hand. They must wait until the Iroquois are close enough so they cannot miss and waste a shot, but not so close they will be overrun. There'll be no time to reload.

The French soldier hangs tied to the tree, burnt and bloody. The screams of the approaching Iroquois wrench him back into consciousness. He moans and writhes in pain and terror.

Brulé picks up a musket and shoots the man in the chest, knowing he will never survive his wounds, or, if he should, what revenge the Iroquois would exact on him. A dozen crows explode out of the trees with the shot, cawing as they cross the clearing. Their screeching, flapping mass separates as a white hawk launches itself from higher up in the trees, drops silently past them, and sweeps across the clearing and starts to climb.

Brulé watches the hawk as he reloads the musket. As he sets the musket down, he notices LeCharon's crucifix in the grass at his feet. He picks it up and hangs it around his neck. "We'll need all the help we can get."

"I suppose it is too late to worry about Heaven or Hell now," says Savignon.

"We'll find Paradise yet, my friend." He sees Brulé's face smeared dark with dirt and blood, but his eyes shine clear, fearless of whatever is to come, either here, or in the hereafter.

The crows resettle in the trees. However this battle unfolds, they at least will be fed.

Just then, the screams of the attacking Iroquois erupt, a barrage of rage and blood lust. The first Iroquois emerge into view, clambering over the boulders at the far end of the long, rock cleft. Brulé shoulders a musket, knowing he will have to wait a bit longer yet before having a sure shot. He gazes up at the hawk. It glides above them, distant, soaring fast, sweeping high above the trees, and then it's gone.

# Afterword

My eighth-grade history teacher, Mr. Carver, fashioned a narrative around Etienne Brulé that brought him to life, and which I never forgot. Something of his life in the wilderness rung true, called to something in me. Each summer I took canoes trips in northern Ontario that further honed that narrative with experiences in the very same wilderness that inspired Brulé.

When I was seventeen on a canoe trip down the Bloodvein River in northern Manitoba, I awoke one morning feeling a deep spiritual peace and joy, in complete contrast to my usual teenage angst and confusion. The feeling resonated to my core, and I associated it with being in the wilderness, with being at one with it. Albert Camus once wrote, a person's "work is nothing but the slow trek to rediscover, through the long detour of art, those two or three great and simple images in whose presence their heart first opened." I experienced that opening on the Bloodvein and it stayed with me. My desire to rediscover that pristine state of simplicity, I projected onto Brulé and the reason he lived with the Wendat.

Decades later, I sat outdoors drinking coffee in Oakville, a town near Toronto, with my friend Jakob de Boer, not far in fact from the long portage the Wendat, and Brulé himself, would have used to go from Lake Ontario to Lake Simcoe. Jakob, a photographer and filmmaker, described a film script he was working on and something in his story reminded me of how I imagined a story about Brulé. I mentioned it and did not get two sentences into my idea before Jakob said, "You have to write this." I said, "Wait, just a minute. I haven't even started". I got two more sentences into it and again, even more emphatically, he said, "You have to write this."

Now lots of people have told me I must do all kinds of things over the years. And I don't. But those words struck deep; they hit some narrative core in me. I began reading and researching everything I could about the Wendat and those early years of the French in the New France, and about writing film scripts. Then I began writing one dreadful script after another as I slowly came to terms with that very specific and demanding art form. A script rests on structure, with two main tools to tell the story — action and dialogue. What can't be filmed — psychology, inner dialogue, abstract ideas — are all out. Only what can be tangibly seen onscreen remains. The scriptwriter also leaves out most description. Except for the most basic outline, all details of costuming, sets and locations will be fleshed out by the costume, set and production designers. The script also leaves out all camera directions, such as close up, or pan to left to reveal the dead body, or whatever. Those directions are the job of the director. If you see a script with those camera directions, it is the shooting script created by the director and cinematographer. A script is one honed piece of structure without much distraction. All story.

Fashioning that script on Brulé took years of writing and rewriting. Actually most screenwriters would probably say they have had that experience at some point in their career. In my case most of that rewriting was in service of learning what a script was—definitely one of those "long detours of art"! It's devilishly difficult. I remember two things said to me during those years that give a sense of it.

When I moved to LA, not because of the script, I remember my brother telling me he'd heard if you are ever at a party in LA and the small talk begins to lag just ask them how their script is going. Meaning everyone either wants to or tries to write one. The other, "Writing a script is like shitting a piano." It ain't easy.

Eventually with the script pretty much as good as I knew how to make it, I gave it to a couple of script doctors, got notes, made changes. Then I made the rounds to a few producers in Canada, got nowhere, put the script in a drawer and got on with something else.

A couple of years later, my friend Don Clark read the script to his wife Jan. I don't remember exactly why they had a copy. When he finished, he called and said, "You have to do something with this script."

I pulled it out of the drawer and gave it to Jim Bonnet, a story consultant here in LA. I spent several days chatting with him and by the end of the week decided to turn the script into a novel, with illustrations. Pretty much what you have in your hands now.

I am aware of the issues of appropriating native culture to advance a story, particularly the story of a white hero. My experience on the Bloodvein River as a teenager offered me an insight into what I thought motivated Brulé to live with the Wendat. His connection is both to the culture and to the land itself. In trying to give form to Brulé and his story I have had to immerse him in a culture I can only guess at. My fictional recreation of that culture has been expressed I hope with the deepest respect for and sensitivity to the issues of appropriating another's culture to serve my own narrative ends.

# Historical Accuracy

Historical fiction needs an historically reasonable setting, but also needs room to bend accuracy for the sake of the story. With that in mind, I think it worth discussing a few points within the story to clarify its historical accuracy.

## Etienne Brulé

Brulé did come to New France in 1609 with Champlain, and Champlain did send him to live with the Wendat the next spring. When he came back to Québec the following year, he had fully embraced the Wendat way of life. He was the first European to go deep, really deep, into the North American wilderness and live with and adopt the native culture. Brulé's natural aptitude for picking up the native languages and dialects, and what I assume, was a love of being out in the wilderness, allowed him to create trust with the Wendat and alliances with other tribes even further afield.

Disappearing into the wilderness and sometimes not reappearing for two or three years at a time, he spent too much time out there to imagine he was developing the fur trade solely for profit. Because of that, he was not entirely reliable to Champlain's ends. Within a couple of years Champlain sent other Frenchmen into the wilderness to live with different tribes to the west to learn their languages, foster alliances and develop trade.

Brulé clearly holds the mantle of hero in my story. And in his years living with the Wendat he did travel hundreds of miles even deeper into what would seem the endless wilds of the New World. He travelled as far as what is now Duluth at the western end of Lake Superior. He's thought to have travelled on to the Mississippi River which is not far to the west and the local tribes would have known it runs far to the south. Although he was probably assessing everywhere he went for furs and trade, he was unusual for the time. As a European explorer he claimed no territory, keep no notes nor made any maps. He embedded himself in the Wendat way of life. But later he crossed paths with Champlain who rejected him as a traitor, ostensibly for having traded with the English. And in the end he was in fact murdered by a Wendat chief. No one knows why.

One possibility presented by Father Sagard, a Jesuit priest who lived with the Wendat and who clearly thought Brulé was damned, was that he'd been killed because of his licentious relations with the Wendat women. That may reflect the Catholic priest's own fixation more than the motives of the Wendat, who did not have many inhibitions around sexual relations.

The other: Brulé had been captured and tortured by the Iroquois, and escaped. Some Wendat may have been suspicious of that escape and speculated he had escaped in exchange for helping the Iroquois create a trading relationship with the French. If true, Brulé perhaps saw a way to redeem himself with Champlain.

If that was the case, then all the Wendat, who survived as the middlemen among the many tribes trading with the French, would have seen the need to do away with such a devastating threat to their livelihood. However, many Wendat were upset at his murder, so perhaps it was just a personal feud with the chief who killed him.

One account had it that whatever Brulé did crossed some line in the Wendat code. He was given a choice, to leave the Wendat, or stay and be killed. He stayed. That dilemma fascinated me, of someone coming to terms with what he truly is and believing in it to such an extent, that he would rather die for that, than return to something, say the values of the French, he had rejected as now foreign. But, that is a very internal dialogue. And being so internal, would have been difficult to navigate as a script. Perhaps that's a story for another time.

Savignon did go to France the year Brulé first went to live with the Wendat. He stayed for three years and helped forge trust and the alliance between the Wendat and the French.

Champlain travelled out to the Wendat in 1615, but never went back.

## Language

I soon found in writing the novel that saying, "Brulé said in Wendat", "Champlain said in French" got tiresome pretty quickly. So I eliminated almost all of it. The Wendat language was close enough to Iroquois that they would understand each other. The only place where the language became really important to the story itself was the conversation between Father LeCharon and the Wendat chief Atironta, where Brulé is acting as interpreter. Here the very words being translated are a problem, i.e. to jail someone, to hang someone, Heaven and so on. I hoped to show the distance that needed to be crossed in order to begin to understand each other.

## Indians

I made of point of never using the word "Indian" in the novel. Partly because some people find it offensive but also because the word was not used to describe the indigenous peoples of North American until the mid-1800s.

In Canada, Indian was changed in the 1970's to First Nations. In the US the terms Indian, Native American, American Indian are used but many indigenous people prefer to call themselves by their tribal name, although even that is often anglicized, e.g. Navajo for Diné. The word Iroquois is of uncertain origin but is not an Iroquois word. Wendat, or Wyandot, was their own name for themselves. Huron, the anglicized name for them, is probably from the Old French "huré" meaning "bristly, unkempt".

The French in the 16th century referred to the native people as savages. Although obviously an extremely offensive term, in French, 'sauvage' meant more like unspoiled nature. "Une région sauvage" meant a wilderness. So the expression didn't really mean, as we would mean today, a barbarian. And Champlain, unusual in the history of Europeans in the New World, did imagine them somehow being integrated into the colonies of New France. But all, of course, predicated on becoming "civilized", meaning having French values and ethics and being Catholic, that is not being "sauvage".

**Guns**

In 1634 the Iroquois would have been buying guns in fact from the Dutch, who had settled in what is now upstate New York. Fort Orange was located where Albany is today. But the big conflict going forward in this part of the New World ultimately was between the French and English, so I decided to keep the number of players within the conflict simple and symmetric for the sake of the story.

The Iroquois and Wendat found the allure of the muskets irresistible.

The guns were expensive and not very accurate by today's standards, but deadly compared to an arrow. The muskets used in the New World in the 17th century were smooth bore, meaning they had no rifling. The musket ball when fired would tend to weave through the air towards its target. In truth someone with a bow and arrow could release two or three arrows in the time it took to load and fire a musket. Before the musket the Iroquois and Wendat used wooden slatted armour in battle to protect themselves from axe blows and arrows. They had no protection from the lethal damage of the musket ball.

For an extremely well researched account of the role guns played among the tribes of North America see *Thundersticks: Firearms and the Violent Transformation of Native America* by David J. Sliverman (The Belknap Press of Harvard University Press, 2016).

## Religion

In my story, Brulé opposed the Jesuits coming in to try and convert the Wendat. In fact the missionaries, first the Récollets, then the Jesuits, were already travelling to the Wendat by 1615. They were keen to live with the Wendat because the Wendat farmed and therefore stayed in one place. The Algonquin tribes around Québec were hunters, nomadic, so living with them was more difficult.

For the French, converting the "heathens" was central to their mission of colonization.

I tried to reconstruct the Wendat relationship with spirit and the land as respectfully as I could. In looking through the filter of several hundred years of our modern European culture, we have demystified our connection to nature. As Descartes said, man is "master and owner of nature." In that view, spirit resides within us, not in the world. The world is ours to do with as we choose. Most aboriginal cultures see spirit existing inside and out, everywhere and in everything, animate and inanimate. We have lost such a resonance with nature that would have been innate with the Wendat.

The Jesuits saw a people without religion, mired in superstition, that needed saving. It is interesting to read William James's definition of a religion from his *The Varieties of Religious Experience*, as the soul "putting itself in a personal relation with the mysterious power of which it feels the presence." Although their religion almost certainly was clouded by superstitions, just as ours are, this idea, I think, would ring true to the experience of a Wendat. I have tried to capture their sense of that presence as best I could in the story.

The Wendat did not convert to Catholicism at first. Yet by 1640 they begin to convert readily. What caused them to change their mind? The answer is primarily disease. Ironically it is the Jesuits that almost certainly brought the various epidemics to the Wendat.

Imagine living in a village of several hundred, with much travel and intermarriage among the dozens of other local villages. The total population of the Wendat estimated by the Jesuits in 1620 was around 30,000. From 1634, when my story unfolds, to 1640, a smallpox epidemic wiped out half the population. Half! Any sense of a spiritual center the people must have felt, any sense of a social order and a stable unfolding for the future, must have been destroyed. One can only imagine they lived in an unfathomable fear and confusion, and it must have left them grasping for any possible solution. The Jesuits offered them Christ and eternal life after death. Certainly they must have imagined they now lived in some kind of accurséd hell.

Their proud valor to fight Iroquois would have been broken. Add to that the Christian ideal of turning the other cheek forced the Wendat to question their blood feuds with the Iroquois.

That long mutual rivalry maintained by the Iroquois and the Wendat for generations ended in the late fall of 1649 when the Iroquois attacked the vastly reduced Wendat. Those that survived the attacks retreated to an island on Georgian Bay, where many starved to death that winter. In the spring the few that remained split into two groups. Three hundred relocated to Québec and about a thousand moved to the western Great Lakes and then eventually south to Kansas and Oklahoma.

Ethnologists consider when a people's language dies, the culture has died. Although efforts are being made to revive the Wendat language now, technically the last person to speak the language died in the early 19th century.

# Acknowledgments

When I began research for the story Bruce Trigger's work on the Wendat, in particular *The Children of Aataentsic*, and David Hackett Fischer's *Champlain's Dream* were invaluable. Channing Gibson, Tom Darro, Jamie McGill, Britt Roberts and Pilar Alessandra all gave thoughtful and helpful suggestions during the writing of the script.

Spending several days talking with Jim Bonnet convinced me the story was worth pursuing as a novel. Vicki Leblanc helped me immensely in crafting the language from script to novel. Guitta Karubian and Jo Rapier I'd like to thank for their careful edits. As well as Alan Teare for his thoughtful reading of the novel for historical detail.

Tom Darro convinced me black and white illustrations would work. Doug Rosman shot hundreds of reference photos for me dressed as Brulé, Savignon and LeCharon. The photos are hilarious and I'll have to post them someday. But they were perfect as reference for the illustrations. Doug also pulled my design ideas for the book into form in InDesign. When he left town to do an MFA, Ari Bharthania helped me with the cover and getting the book ready for the printer.

Above all during the years I worked on this my wife, Anne Ward, and our kids Emily and Claire have offered a loving and beautiful home — a land apart. Thank you.

Ian Roberts went landscape painting with his father from the age of 11. Later he attended the New School of Art and the Ontario College of Art, both in Toronto. He has painted ever since. But this story about Etienne Brulé percolated inside him since he was a teenager canoeing in the woods of northern Ontario and one day just started coming out. He is the author of two other books, *Creative Authenticity, 16 Principles to Clarify Your Artistic Vision*, also published by Atelier Saint-Luc Press and *Mastering Composition* (North Light Books), which has sold over 40,000 copies. As well he has produced numerous instructional videos on painting. He lives in Los Angeles with his wife, the painter, Anne Ward.

ianroberts.com